Everything's Under Control

WILLOW CREEK BOOK #1

CARRIE JACOBS

for IAA, for obvious reasons
*looks directly at camera**

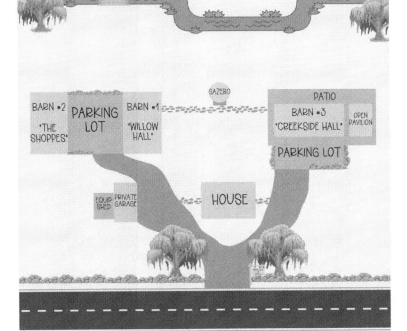

Chapter One

Two outs, no one on base, middle of the fifth with a score of 1-0 in favor of the home team Chicago Cubs. Summer Sullivan arched her back in the molded plastic seat, trying to get comfortable. Her sort-of boyfriend, celebrity chef Michael Mastriano, was busy preening for a fan several rows over who was not-so-subtly recording him with her phone.

"I'm going to the restroom."

He jerked his attention to her and grabbed her arm. "No, wait. It'll just be a minute."

Typical Michael, completely ignoring or overruling whatever she said or needed. "I have to pee." Celebrity chef or not, it was time to tell him she didn't want to see him anymore. They had nothing in common, and after a handful of months, it was clear this was going nowhere.

The batter whiffed his third strike and jogged back toward the dugout. The fielders ran in as the visiting team headed out to their places on the field.

"Any second now."

"What?"

Michael wasn't looking at her. His eyes were glued to the

left field jumbotron. He still gripped her arm, and with his other hand, he fumbled in the pocket of his designer jeans.

"What are you—"

A deafening cheer filled the stadium.

"Ha! There it is!" Michael pointed to left field.

Summer looked where he was pointing. The giant screen flashed, "WILL YOU MARRY ME SUMER?" Digital hearts popped around the words.

She immediately smiled. Wasn't that nice. She craned her neck, looking to see if she could spot the happy couple.

Wait.

Hang on.

Sumer? Was that supposed to say Summer? Her giant confused face appeared on screens all around the stadium.

Oh, crap. She snapped her attention back to Michael and quickly faked a smile. He pointed to the camera, then dramatically dropped to one knee and held out a ring box.

"Well? What do you say?"

What *could* she say with forty thousand pairs of eyeballs glued to her reaction? An intimidating number of those forty thousand people began chanting, "SAY YES! SAY YES! SAY YES!" Sudden claustrophobia joined the party, and it felt like the crowd was crushing in on her.

Michael impatiently jammed the ring on her finger without waiting for an answer.

Summer mentally shook herself. *Get it under control, Summer. Freak out later.* She flashed a big smile that she hoped didn't look as fake as it felt, and a thumbs up to the camera. The crowd went wild. She let Michael jump up and hug her. She got a faceful of gel-stiff hair because he was still making eyes at the camera.

The screen flipped to a happy birthday message for twins

Cody and Coby, thankfully taking the attention away from them, at least for the moment.

Summer kept a smile plastered on her face. She always did when she was in public with Michael, because the paparazzi followed him everywhere. The downside of dating a celebrity chef. *One* of the downsides. Without moving her lips, she asked, "What the heck was that?"

He kept smiling and leaned his head close to hers. "I told you the Family Network didn't want to move forward until my private life was a little more family-friendly."

"You ambushed me."

"Babe, come on."

"Michael, we didn't even talk about this."

"Babe, it's just business. Besides, I wanted your reaction to be genuine."

Summer huffed a humorless laugh. Business? Marriage shouldn't have anything to do with business. "It wasn't, though."

"What do you mean? I totally surprised you." He still wasn't looking directly at her.

"I mean I wouldn't have said yes."

His head finally swiveled to face her. His expression was genuinely baffled. "What?"

Summer was baffled at his bafflement. "We've been casually dating for like four months. We've never had a single conversation about being exclusive, let alone getting married."

He blinked a few times. "Of course you want to marry me. I'm *Michael Mastriano*." He tapped his chest and shrugged like that made it a done deal.

The crowd surged to its feet, erupting with screams and cheers. Summer stood along with everyone else, clapping as the Cubs nailed a triple play, driving the score to 4-0. Arms raised into the air all around the stadium. The people in front of them high-fived. Someone a few seats away shrieked as the guy behind them spilled beer down their back.

She took advantage of the chaos and leaned over to Michael. "I really have to pee."

"Sure, babe. Bring me a beer," he said without looking at her.

Summer jogged up the concrete stairs and out into the concourse. She headed toward the restroom, planning to take a breath and regroup before heading back inside. Her feet had another idea and took her past the restrooms. Instead, she tugged her Cubs cap down a little and veered to the sloping concrete walkway that led to the ground floor. She slowed long enough to tap into an app on her phone, then hustled to the exit. Instinctively, she twisted the ring so the massive diamond was in her palm and not attracting attention from any would-be thieves.

She fell in with the flow of people leaving the game early and slipped out the main gate. She double checked her app and scanned the cars waiting at the curb. It only took a second to verify the license plate for her Uber, then she hopped into the back seat.

The car zipped away from the curb. They had left Addison St. and turned onto Ashland Ave. before her phone buzzed with an incoming text from Michael. Her heart pounded. Did he know she left? How mad was he?

> Where's my beer?

Apparently not. She wondered if he noticed her missing, or just realized he hadn't gotten the beer he requested.

She leaned toward the driver's seat. "Can you go any faster?"

The driver shot an annoyed look in the rear-view mirror. He probably heard that from every fare he picked up.

"Sorry." She settled back against the seat, tapping her fingers on her knee. The ring was ridiculous. A huge sparkly diamond surrounded by slightly less-huge sparkly diamonds. It probably cost more than three years' rent for her nice apartment.

She tried to make sense of the situation. In four months, she and Michael had only seen each other in person a handful of times and barely communicated between his trips to the city. It was nothing serious. They'd never discussed being serious, and they'd certainly never discussed marriage. In fact, the only thing they ever really *had* discussed was Michael Mastriano.

This wasn't some one-sided situation – he clearly wasn't very into her, either. But somehow, this was all going to blow up in her face, she just knew it.

Twenty minutes and a lot of turns later, the car lurched to a stop in front of Michael's gorgeous brownstone row home.

"Thanks," Summer said as she got out.

"Leave a good tip!" the driver shouted as he sped off.

She'd deal with that later on the app. For now, she let herself into Michael's apartment. She hadn't wanted to accept the key, but now she was glad he'd insisted on giving it to her. She quickly gathered her backpack she'd left there for safekeeping during the game. She slipped the ring off her finger and set it on the kitchen counter with his key. Just in case, she snapped a picture, then hustled outside and locked the door behind her.

Her own apartment was fifteen blocks away in a far less posh section of the city. She debated ordering another Uber, but the early September afternoon was warm and clear, and she'd rather get moving than wait around.

As her sneakers slapped along the pavement, she adjusted

the shoulder straps of her backpack. What the heck just happened? Why hadn't Michael even mentioned this scheme of his? Oh, right, because she was a supporting character in the show of his life. No, not even a supporting character. More like an extra.

It stung a little that it wasn't some fascinating part of her personality he found irresistible. Nope, it was the fact that she had a squeaky clean reputation and he was hoping that would rub off on him. Or, more accurately, he was hoping the Family Network would be swayed by her reputation. Gross.

She kept her gaze forward and her stride steady. Growing up in a small town hadn't adequately prepared her for city streets. Even walking through a relatively safe neighborhood had her vigilance on high alert.

Since meeting Michael, that was a near-constant state. She'd been the subject of countless trash clickbait articles and a few viral TikToks that dragged her through the mud as not good enough for America's sweetheart chef, Michael Mastriano.

Originally from Italy, he was tall, dark, handsome, and incredibly full of himself. His food was amazing. His conversation? Not so much.

Summer was honest with herself. If he hadn't been *Michael Mastriano*, she wouldn't have gone on a second date after he'd spent the entire first date talking about himself and called her "Shumer" twice, but she supposed she was as vulnerable to the dazzling allure of fame as anyone else, and attention from him was a pretty substantial ego boost. After all, he was *Michael Mastriano*, as he frequently pointed out. At least now she knew why he'd asked her out in the first place, then kept her around when he had access to a full stable of beautiful women at the drop of a hat. Tall ones.

Not like she was a bridge troll, but Summer couldn't hold a

candle to the runway model type Michael was usually photographed with, especially since she clocked in at five-foot-three if she stretched to her full height. With shoes on.

She turned the corner onto her block and picked up the pace. All she wanted was to get inside her apartment and put this day behind her.

"Well, well, well."

Summer froze. She'd know that nails-on-the-chalkboard voice anywhere. She turned slowly and faced Nina Hardwick, trash journalist.

"I zipped right over here to offer my congratulations, but..." Nina gestured to the empty sidewalk with her perfectly manicured blood red nails. Fitting. "I see you're heading to your apartment alone." She made a big show of bending down to inspect Summer's hand. "Without a ring. Hmm. Whatever could this mean?"

"Ring? What— How do you know anything about a ring?" She clamped her lips together. She'd already said too much.

"Aww, you sweet *summer* child," Nina snarked with more artificial sweetness than a Sweet 'N Low factory. "I happened to tune into the game at just the right time to see none other than Michael Mastriano dipping onto one knee in front of you." The last word dripped contempt. "I kept watching and the next time the camera panned back to that dreamy culinary genius, I saw your empty seat, and I thought to myself, now *why* is her seat empty?"

"Nina—"

"After your pathetic lukewarm acceptance, I had a hunch you hadn't just run to the ladies' room, so I popped right over here quick as I could, and what do you know, my hunch was correct." One perfectly manicured eyebrow arched upward slightly, struggling against the Botox. "As usual."

Summer hated the way this woman in particular got under

her skin. She'd shown up in a group of paparazzi at her first date with Michael and had apparently made it her personal mission to drive Summer bonkers. "Nina—"

Nina held up a finger and tapped onto her phone. "My goodness. Michael Mastriano just posted a picture announcing your engagement." Her eyes danced with amusement as she turned the phone to show Summer.

The picture was completely on brand. It was a picture of Michael, by himself, announcing his engagement. Summer wasn't even tagged in the photo.

Nina laughed with authentic glee. "He doesn't know he's been dumped yet. Wow. I love getting a scoop, but this is just too good. You should tell me your side, Summer."

"No comment." Until recently, she thought only super-heroes had arch-nemeses, but apparently mild-mannered wedding planners could have them, too.

Nina shrugged one shoulder and snapped a picture before Summer could move. "Doesn't matter. 'A source close to the couple' will fill in the blanks." Her talons scratched air quotes around the words.

"You could just leave it alone."

Her laugh held genuine amusement. "Oh, come on, Summer. Would you walk past a stack of cash on your doorstep? Because that's what you've given me." The eyebrow struggled upward again. "You sure you don't want to give me your side? I can have everyone on #TeamSummer with one post. One juicy tidbit is all it takes. Is Michael cheap? Bad in bed? An alcoholic? Broke? Gave someone food poisoning? Come on, Summer, you might as well get on the right side of this."

"No, thank you." She didn't want to be on *any* side of this.

Nina lifted her phone and snapped another picture. "Suit yourself."

Summer ran up the steps and covered the keypad with one hand as she punched in her code with the other. The door's lock mechanism clicked and she pushed into the building.

She'd barely gotten into her apartment when her phone vibrated with the short-short-long sequence she'd assigned to her boss, the notorious wedding industry giant, Reesa Flynn.

"Hello—"

Reesa interrupted her. "Did you just dump Michael Mastriano on national television?"

"What? No." How would Reesa know? Was she in cahoots with Nina? Because she certainly didn't watch baseball.

"Look, Summer, I thought you understood that Michael Mastriano was *good for your position* here." She enunciated the words deliberately.

Well, yeah. He had fifty million devoted followers, so of course he'd be good for business. "Sure, I know his visibility would be good for the company, but—"

"Our high-value brides want to trust their planner, Summer. They'll be clawing each other out of the way to get to work with the planner who's taking care of the high-profile wedding for Michael Mastriano. We'd be booked for years, Summer. *Years.*"

Summer dropped her backpack onto the couch and sank down into the cushion beside it. It wasn't lost on her that Reesa didn't mention that it would be *her* wedding, too. "You knew Michael was going to propose?" It wasn't really a question.

There was an annoyed beat of silence before Reesa snapped, "Of course I knew. It was my idea. It's a win-win for all of us. Michael gets to make over his playboy image for the Family Network, we get a big fat payday and tons of exposure to plan his wedding, and you get to be the wife of the hottest chef on the planet. Do you know how many brides will want you to plan their weddings?"

Her head spun. It felt so gross to be an unwitting pawn in someone else's chess game. "Reesa, I can't marry Michael Mastriano."

"For Pete's sake, marry him and then have a nice, quiet divorce in a couple years. You could even squirt out a kid or two and have a steady income stream that way."

Summer couldn't believe what she was hearing. "I'm not going to participate in a sham marriage." Marriage wasn't a joke. It was supposed to be sacred. One time, for life. Not to mention the fact that she couldn't "squirt out a kid" even if she wanted to.

Reesa's voice turned cold. "I'm sorry to hear that."

"I don't understand. I'm the best planner on the team. You've said yourself that my work is flawless and my attention to detail is impeccable." All true, and Reesa didn't hand out compliments lightly. In fact, Reesa herself assigned every new planner to work under Summer, no matter how impressive their resume was coming in.

"But you hit the key word, Summer. Team. All that good work is meaningless if you aren't a team player."

Summer pinched the bridge of her nose and squeezed her eyes shut. "I'm not a team player because I won't marry Michael Mastriano? That has nothing to do with my work."

"You do catch on quick."

Summer flopped back on the couch and stared up at the ceiling. With no job, she wouldn't be able to make rent. Would being Mrs. Mastriano really be so bad? No. She wasn't going to sell her soul for this ridiculous scheme. She could make a few calls and see what other jobs were out there. With her talent and long list of happy brides, many of whom Reesa considered "high value," it should be easy enough to land another great job.

Reesa interrupted her thoughts. "And before you think you

can take your skills to a competitor, understand that I'll make sure no one in Chicago will be willing to work with you."

"Why are you doing this to me?" At least she could understand Michael's motivation for using her.

Reesa gave an impatient huff. "It's not about you. It's about securing Michael as part of this company."

It still didn't make sense. None of the other employees' spouses were involved. Unless... The answer clicked. "He was going to invest. You give me over on a silver platter to fix his image, and he injects a bunch of cash into his new wife's job." Now it made a lot more sense why Michael was interested in her, a nobody from the middle of nowhere. A real Cinderella story. That stung.

"Bravo. You'll reconsider your position and clean up this mess."

Summer's phone began vibrating like crazy and she heard Reesa's phone pinging. That couldn't be good.

"Reesa, I—"

"Never mind. One of the interns will clean out your office." The line went dead.

Her friend Kayla, who also worked for Reesa, texted her.

> What's going on? I heard Reesa say she fired you?????????

Summer turned her phone off and went to take a hot shower. Maybe this would all blow over by the time she was done.

When she was dressed again, her hair wrapped in a fuzzy towel, she felt marginally better. Until she saw Kayla's next text. A screenshot of Michael Mastriano's dramatic post about how Summer had crushed his soul and broken his heart. She swiped onto social media and found his post. He'd taken a selfie where he stared artistically off into the outfield. He'd even used a filter that added tears to his eyes. Oh, and this time, the jerk *had* tagged her. In under thirty minutes, he had almost a quarter of a million reactions and hundreds upon hundreds of posts from women offering to ease his pain any way he wanted. Barf.

Her own phone started going bananas. The nonstop vibrations from texts and social media notifications were unbearable after a few minutes. She figured the best thing she could do was ignore them and lay low until something else went viral and people forgot she existed. It couldn't take long, could it?

But when she logged back into her social media to mute the notifications, she noticed a disturbing amount of violent threats, made all the more frightening by the fact someone had doxxed her, complete with a picture of her building. A cold shiver ran down her spine. Why would anyone care about any of this? Why wouldn't they be glad she'd turned him down to slip back into the obscurity she'd come from?

Her building was secure for the most part, but she still packed an overnight bag in case she had to go to a hotel. She nearly jumped out of her skin when the intercom buzzed at eight thirty.

She checked the video intercom and leaned against the wall in relief when she saw Kayla. She buzzed her in and watched at the peephole until Kayla came into view in front of her door.

"Are you okay?"

Her "yes" was automatic, and not accurate at all. "No. I don't know."

Kayla set a box on the kitchen table.

Reesa hadn't been playing around. In a matter of hours, Summer's entire career had been distilled down to a single cardboard box with her personal items carelessly tossed inside.

"She didn't let me clean your office out. Sorry." Kayla gave her a sympathetic smile.

Summer rummaged through the box. It ticked her off that some things were missing that she'd brought with her when she took the job, like the binders with swatches she'd put together and her favorite color wheel, but neither was valuable enough or irreplaceable enough to poke the hornet's nest by calling Reesa.

"I guess I have to kiss my binders goodbye."

"I'll see if I can find them, but no promises. You know I love you, but... Reesa." She made a sour face.

"No, don't stick your neck out for me." It stung how relieved Kayla looked. Not that she could blame her.

"What happened?"

Summer hated that she was a little suspicious of her friend. They'd worked together for five years under Reesa, commiserating at their evil *Devil Wears Prada*-level boss. But she was also smart enough to know that Kayla's livelihood depended on Reesa's whims, just like hers. The inside scoop was always valuable currency.

She kept it to what was already out there. "I don't know. Michael Mastriano proposed to me at the game out of the blue. I didn't really answer. Kinda went with it for the camera. Then I booked it out of the stadium and left the ring at his place. I came home and Nina Hardwick jumped out of a cab and asked me for the scoop."

"Whoa. How'd she know anything that fast?"

"She *said* she was watching the game, but she doesn't really seem the type to watch baseball. There's always paparazzi following Michael Mastriano, so I'm guessing one of them tipped her off." It only now occurred to her that she always referred to him by his first and last name. One more clue that their entire relationship had been a sham.

"Where do you think you'll try getting in? With your resume, it shouldn't be too hard. Maybe Sachman's?"

Once again, Summer found herself suspicious and frustrated because she had no idea if she had any reason to be. "Who knows. If all else fails, I have experience as a barista." She forced a smile.

Kayla glanced toward the door. "I really hate to rush off—"

She got it. Kayla didn't want to be on the wrong side of Reesa's wrath. "No, it's fine. I'm fine. Who knows who might be lurking around and reporting back to Reesa."

"I'm really sorry."

Summer didn't know what she was apologizing for, but it didn't matter much. "Thanks for bringing my stuff."

"Of course." Kayla looked like she wanted to say more, but in the end, she didn't.

Summer closed the door behind her and turned both locks. It hurt.

She told herself not to, but she couldn't stay off social media. The horrible messages, public and private, kept coming, and some of them were downright scary. Even some of her so-called friends were posting replies to posts with nasty messages about her gold digging ways that were backed up with zero facts, because it was ludicrous.

After her talk with Reesa, reading the hateful messages, and overanalyzing Kayla's squirrely demeanor, she wasn't sure there was a single person in Chicago she could trust.

Instead, she called the one person in the world she knew she could always count on. The one person who would have her back no matter what. The one person who picked up every time she called, without fail.

As soon as the call connected, Summer burst into relieved tears.

"Mom? I think I need to come home."

Chapter Two

Ten days later, Summer rolled down the door of the U-Haul and secured the latch. She winced as a box toppled over and crashed somewhere inside the truck.

The teenage boys from her building who'd helped carry everything both took a step back. "That's not our fault."

Summer managed a tired smile. "It's fine. Thanks so much for helping."

The boys had asked for fifty bucks apiece, but she handed them each a hundred dollars. It was a fraction of what she'd have paid professional movers, and she was grateful for their help – and their kindness. She hadn't seen much of that this past week and a half.

The building's door clicked shut behind the boys and it hurt a little to realize she couldn't go back in if she wanted to. She loved her homey apartment with the little balcony, her quiet neighbors, and even the little yappy dog from the third floor who managed to get himself trapped in the elevator at least once a month.

The past week and a half had been the most rushed and frustrating of her life. The horrible messages had slowed to a trickle, but Nina made sure the topic of Michael Mastriano's broken heart stayed front and center.

Reesa made good on her threat, because not a single company Summer reached out to would even take her calls. She'd been swiftly and effectively blacklisted, for absolutely no reason.

Worst of all, someone had broken into her building's private parking garage and vandalized her vehicle, scratching foul words deep into the paint. Rather than cooperate with the police, hand over surveillance footage, and involve their insurance company, the landlord told her to vacate the premises. So instead of using the money in her savings account for the next month's rent, she spent it on a U-Haul to get from Chicago back to Central Pennsylvania.

Back to Willow Creek.

Thankfully the landlord wasn't completely soulless. The building manager had done the walkthrough and handed her a check for her full security deposit and a refund of the prorated rent she'd already paid for the remaining two weeks of September, along with making her sign a not-so-subtle, "This completes our obligation so don't bother trying to sue us" notice.

Thanks to her newfound lack of trust in anyone or anything, she cashed the check immediately before they could stop payment on it. Not that she thought they'd go to the trouble, but then again, she never would have expected Reesa to arrange a sham marriage and then fire her for refusing to go through with it, or that she'd be getting death threats and property damage from the rabid fans of a celebrity chef.

The day was dreary and chilly, and the road was long. On I90, she white-knuckled the steering wheel for an hour, navigating scarily aggressive traffic, praying the trailer holding her beloved Ford Escape stayed attached to the U-Haul. Once she made it past Gary, Indiana, the urban scenery finally gave up in favor of fields and small towns. The highway skirted around South Bend, toed the Michigan state line, then dipped down into Ohio.

A few minutes into Ohio, she left the highway and stopped for gas and lunch at a lonely Love's travel plaza with an attached Arby's. She wolfed down the last of her curly fries dipped in Arby's sauce and headed back onto the highway.

She passed Toledo. Somewhere around Cleveland, I90 became I80. At suppertime, she stopped at a nice hotel near Youngstown, Ohio, close to the Pennsylvania state line. The clerk at the front desk barely acknowledged her, so that was a plus. After the past two weeks, being invisible was a blessing. She'd gotten some openly curious looks and pointed fingers at the first rest stop, but hopefully all the drama stayed behind her. Another plus was the robust room service menu. She treated herself to too much food so she could eat her feelings in peace while watching a marathon of *The Office* reruns. After the week she'd had, she deserved the indulgence.

The bed was reasonably comfortable, but she tossed and turned most of the night. Had it really only been ten days since her life was flipped upside down? It felt like so much longer.

In the morning, she stood in the hot shower as long as she could. Her shoulders and back ached from packing and lifting and driving. She crammed her dirty clothes into her bag and toweled her hair. It was still damp when she tied it back in a ponytail. Leggings and an oversized sweatshirt was the wardrobe of choice for the day.

Her phone dinged with a text from Kayla.

I got your binders. They're a little rough.
Should I bring them over?

She felt a twinge of guilt that she hadn't spoken to Kayla or told her she was leaving.

> I'm heading back to PA. Can you mail them? I'll cashapp you for the shipping.

> Wait. Are you leaving for good????

> Didn't have a lot of choice.

She pulled in a deep breath and sent another message.

> I'm sorry I didn't tell you. It's been crazy and I had to get out of Chicago.

> I don't blame you. Stay in touch, ok?? I'll ship your stuff, lmk the address.

She sent another message with a string of heart emojis.

> Thank you so much. I'll call you when I get home.

Home. She'd been close to feeling like Chicago was home, but leaving didn't hurt as much as it might have, so maybe it wasn't home after all. She texted Kayla the address of the farm.

She took advantage of the hotel's generous continental breakfast, filling up on scrambled eggs, bacon, fresh fruit, and coffee that would hopefully get her through the last four hour leg of this trip.

She checked out and walked across the parking lot. Her Ford Escape was secured on a low trailer, hitched to the U-Haul. The words scratched along the passenger side of her vehicle looked even worse in the bright morning light. At least there was a silver lining to paying a small fortune for full coverage insurance. With any luck, she'd only be out her deductible.

Making her way across Pennsylvania, Philipsburg seemed like a good midway point for a break. She stopped at Sheetz for gas, a stretch, and a large caffeine.

The last leg of the trip was uneventful until she passed State College and hit the Seven Mountains. In the biggest, heaviest vehicle she'd ever driven, with all her worldly possessions in tow. Cars and tractor trailers whipped past her down the steep incline. She hated traveling this section of road in a regular car, and the seven years she'd spent in Chicago meant not driving on mountain roads at all. That was probably the best thing about the city. Okay, that and the deep dish.

The U-Haul handled the road just fine. Summer did not.

The runaway truck ramp did nothing to soothe her nerves as she white-knuckled the steering wheel and rode the brakes down, down, down and around, around, around.

When she reached the bottom of the mountain, the tense jitters were nearly unbearable. She made another quick stop at the Sheetz in Reedsville, just to get out of the truck and walk off some of the anxious energy. Most of it was from coming down the mountain and feeling like the brakes would fail and she'd somehow careen through the concrete barrier, cross both lanes of oncoming traffic, and fly off the mountain into the river. But some of it was from being only half an hour away from home.

Summer wanted to go home, but at the same time, she dreaded it. She walked around the U-Haul and then went inside to use the restroom. All that tension had worked its way to her bladder. She bought a bottle of water she didn't really want because she felt bad about using the restroom without purchasing anything.

Back in the U-Haul, she clicked her seatbelt into place and got back on Route 322 for the last part of her drive.

Just before eleven thirty, Summer turned onto the back road that would take her to Willow Creek. A few minutes after that, the twin weeping willows and low stone walls that flanked the driveway to the farm came into view.

Summer blinked back tears, not sure if they were from relief or not. Probably. She put on her turn signal and pulled the U-Haul onto the driveway, carefully checking her mirrors to make sure the trailer holding her vehicle didn't scrape the stone wall.

The elegant "Welcome to Willow Creek" sign swung awkwardly, dangling from one corner. The chain that secured the other corner was rusted and broken.

She slowed the truck and frowned. Weeds climbed along the stone wall, covering their beauty. The grass along the driveway rustled in the breeze, much too long for what was normally a perfectly manicured lawn.

Before she could think too much about the state of the vegetation, movement caught her eye. Her mom stood on the front porch, waving. A shutter was missing from one of the upstairs windows.

She hit the gas and headed for the house.

Chapter Three

Ben Keller took a step backwards into the shadows of the garage as the U-Haul lumbered slowly up the driveway. So it was true. Summer was back.

The U-Haul stopped and the engine turned off. Summer jumped out and ran up the porch steps and tackled her mother in a bear hug. Andi beamed, with tears rolling down her cheeks.

A lot of thoughts played in his mind. She looked great. It had been seven, maybe eight years since he'd seen her in person. Her hair was long, pulled into a ponytail that went halfway down her back, dark with some highlighted streaks. Her smile was genuine, but didn't quite reach her red, tired-looking eyes. Probably a combination of the long drive and the bad situation.

He'd been watching baseball with his dad a few weeks ago on a random Saturday afternoon, when Charlie pointed at the screen and said, "Holy cow, that's our Summer!"

Ben had been so stunned a chip loaded with salsa fell out of his hand and left a splotchy red stain down the front of his favorite white Cubs t-shirt. His heart had squeezed for her. She looked trapped, even though she smiled for the cameras.

From there, he'd been unable to stop following the unfolding drama online, watching in real time as Summer's pristine reputation was shredded to something irreparable, and there was nothing he could do to stop it. Once, twice, a dozen times, his finger hovered over her number in his phone, but he was afraid it would make her feel worse to know everyone back home knew what was happening to her.

He couldn't blame her for leaving Chicago. He'd have run back home, too.

The sun glinted off her SUV on the U-Haul trailer. He walked over and let out a low whistle as he read the foul words someone had carved into the paint. Andi went back inside the house as Summer came down off the porch and walked in his direction.

"Well, well, well, if it isn't Ben-Dover." She grinned, even though her eyes were red from crying.

"Well, well, well, if it isn't Summer Breeze Between Her Ears." He matched her smile and didn't refuse when she came in for a hug. He squeezed her and let go. Even though he didn't really want to.

"How are you?" she asked.

"Better than you, it sounds like. Are you okay?" He stepped away from her and ran a finger across the scratches in the blue paint.

"Who, me? Better than okay. Living the dream." She shook her fists in the air and laughed a little, but Ben could see the hurt underneath the humor.

"You need help unloading?"

She bit her lip. "I kind of need help unloading twice." She held up two fingers. "Just a few boxes here, and then the rest is going into my storage unit."

Footsteps crunched on the gravel. "Summer!"

She whirled around. "Gavin!"

"I've missed you, rotten brat." Gavin opened his arms and bent forward.

"I've missed you, too, stupid jerk." Summer flung herself into her brother's arms.

Ben hung back as they bear-hugged. "I'll put the tractor away, then I can help you unload."

He didn't wait for a response. Summer and Gavin were two peas in a pod, and it had been too long since their last visit. The riding mower roared back to life as he turned the key. He drove it around the side of the garage, back to the equipment shed's open door and parked it inside. The mowing was already behind, another day wouldn't make a difference.

His stomach knotted. Obviously he wasn't as over Summer Sullivan as he swore up and down he was. He blew out a puff of air and walked back to the truck.

Gavin rolled the U-Haul's door up. "What needs to go in the house?"

Summer tapped a stack of boxes. "These, and those suitcases. I was tempted to put it all at the back so you'd have to unload the whole truck and reload it, but see? I can be nice."

"You got a concussion?" Gavin teased.

"You'd know all about brain damage, wouldn't you?" She fired back.

"Now, now, children," Ben said. He grabbed a box and carried it to the porch. "Might as well put everything here, then take it upstairs?"

"Here, put it inside," Andi said, holding the front door wide open. "We can take everything upstairs after lunch."

Ben obeyed, putting the box near the foot of the staircase.

Soon, Summer's boxes and suitcases were piled neatly,

waiting to be moved to her childhood bedroom that had long since been converted to a guest room.

"Can you guys help me take the rest of the stuff to storage?"

Andi waved her hand. "Lunch first. You've been traveling for two days, and I'm sure you didn't eat anything decent."

"Not true," Summer argued. "I had a really nice breakfast this morning at the hotel."

Andi arched an eyebrow. "Lunch. All of you."

Just like he did when they were kids, Ben fell in line behind Gavin and followed Andi to the kitchen, where she plied them with a salad full of veggies from the last harvest of her garden, ham sandwiches, and leftover macaroni and cheese.

"Where's everybody else?" Summer asked as she ate.

Andi swallowed. "Jillian took your dad and Nana into town for doctors' appointments. They should be back before long."

Ben teased, "They were smart enough to not be here when you rolled up."

"Oh, big surprise they're smarter than you," she answered.

Gavin leaned back and gave a loud belly laugh. "Don't be getting on a high horse about being smart. Weren't you just run out of Chicago?"

Andi scolded him, "Leaving all that nonsense behind and coming home was very smart."

Ben had to agree. He'd seen some of the hit pieces Nina Hardwick had put out, which her nasty minions then spread, embellishing along the way.

Even though the "proposal" was on film, easily accessible, the story had grown into Evil Heartless Summer slapping the ring out of Michael Mastriano's hand and spitting in his face, leaving America's Culinary Sweetheart devastated and weeping on his knees in the stands of Wrigley Stadium, never to recover.

Ben had no idea what the real story was, but he knew it wasn't that. He'd watched the clip a few times. Okay, several dozen times. He knew Summer well enough to know the smile she'd flashed at the camera was her "get me out of here" smile.

It was not the happy, excited smile of a woman who expected or wanted a proposal on national television in the middle of a Cubs game. And for Summer's job to be affected? There was way more to the story that hadn't made it to the online gossip rags.

"Ready to go show off those muscles?" Summer tweaked his arm, yanking him out of his thoughts.

"Not me, I'm just going along to supervise." He grinned as he jumped up and pushed his chair in.

They put their dirty dishes in the sink, earning a nod of approval from Andi. "Be careful."

"Yes, Mom," all three of them answered.

Outside, Ben gestured to the SUV on the trailer. "Are we unloading this now?"

Summer answered, "I figured we'd do it after since no one can drive the U-Haul but me."

Ben saw her wince at the nasty words scratched into the paint. "Idea. Why don't you follow me, we'll drop your car off at Gino's, then go unload the U-Haul."

"Gino's?"

"Body shop. Good friend of mine. If anybody can fix this, he can."

Gavin agreed. "Gino's good."

Her shoulders dropped as if talking about the scratches made them impossible to ignore. "Sure. Then you can drop me off at the car rental place, if you don't mind."

Gavin slung his arm around her. "Chin up. You're home now. We've got your back here."

Ben reached over and patted her shoulder. "He's right."

Her chin quivered for a second, but she quickly straightened and gave them a quick nod. "Thanks, boys. Now let's get going."

Ben walked over and got into his truck. He waited while Summer drove up to the big parking lot between Willow Hall, the farm's original barn, and The Shoppes, a second barn that had been added years ago and now housed the farm office, Gavin's bakery, and Jillian's flower shop. She slowly turned the U-Haul around and came back down the lane. Ben pulled out onto the main road and led her toward Gino's.

He drove on auto-pilot, seeing the tailgate of her SUV in his mind. What kind of weirdo was so dedicated to a celebrity chef that they took it this personally when he got dumped? And then went out and committed vandalism in what? His honor? Freaks.

He put his turn signal on well ahead of the crappy dirt lane that took them to Gino's. The body shop was a sketchy-looking little cinder block garage, but Gino was a good friend of Ben's, and he did excellent body work.

Ben jumped out of his vehicle and waved at Gino, who was curiously looking out from under a car he had on a lift inside the open garage.

"Yo, Ben, what's up?"

"We have a little situation."

Gino tossed a wrench onto the massive toolbox along the wall and came out, wiping his hands down the front of his stained coveralls.

Ben pointed to the SUV on the trailer.

Gino let out a low whistle as he bent and closely inspected the scratches. He looked up at Summer. "Whoa. You the wife or the side chick?"

Summer rolled her eyes. "Neither."

Gino snapped his fingers and nodded. "Oh yeah. You're the one from the internet with the chef."

Ben nudged Gino's arm with his elbow. "Sore subject."

"Sure, sure." He turned his attention back to the SUV and ran his fingers along the scratches on the driver's side doors. "These ones aren't too bad. Probably buff right out." He walked around the back and touched the letter W. "This one's pretty deep, though. I'll do what I can, but it might mean stripping it all the way down and repainting." He walked around the other side. "These aren't too bad, either. Back's the worst."

"I have insurance," Summer said.

Gino was still looking at her vehicle. "At least they didn't smash out your lights or windows. Usually when they have this kind of time, they do more damage. What's your deductible?"

"Five hundred." It hadn't occurred to her to feel lucky they'd "only" scratched up her paint.

"Kay. You just want an estimate, or you want me to fix it?"

Summer looked over at Ben.

He said, "It's up to you. If it was me, I'd leave it here."

"Then that's what we'll do. How long will you need it?"

"Probably a week, maybe two."

Ben watched the emotions play across her face. She was probably most worried about being trapped at the house with her parents. It couldn't be easy to come home and navigate that relationship as an adult child staying in her old childhood bedroom.

"Okay. Thanks."

He helped Gino unstrap the vehicle from the trailer, then got the keys from Summer and backed it off. He handed the keys to Gino and glanced back to make sure Summer was out of earshot. "You don't happen to have a loaner or anything, do you? It'd really help her out."

"For a friend of yours, sure," Gino said mildly. He called to Summer, "Can you drive a stick?"

"No."

"Oh." He thought for a minute. "I got an '86 Grand Am you can drive for free as long as you put gas in it. Little rough, but it'll get you from Point A to Point B for a week." He snickered. "As long as Point A isn't too far away from Point B."

Summer stood straighter. "Really? If I don't have to rent a car, that would be amazing."

Ben watched some of the tension leave her face. What would a rental car cost, anyway? At least a couple hundred bucks, and even if insurance reimbursed the cost, they'd surely take their sweet time.

"Let's do some paperwork and I'll get you the key."

She reached out and grabbed Ben's hand on her way past, giving it a quick squeeze. "Thank you."

He shrugged it off like it was nothing. No big deal.

This whole thing was no big deal, right? So what if Summer Sullivan just rolled back into town? His best friend's big sister is all she ever was. Even if he'd ever had the nerve to tell her he hoped for more, it was unlikely she felt the same.

So why did his hand tingle from her touch?

Chapter Four

The tailpipe of the Grand Am backfired like it had launched a cannonball. The inside smelled like twenty-year-old French fries and motor oil, but Gino was right. It got her from Point A to Point B. And it was free, so she wasn't going to complain about aesthetics.

After they returned the U-Haul and got back to the farm, Summer said, "I thought Ben would be back before us."

Gavin shrugged as he got out of the car. "Probably went to work."

That didn't make sense. "Work? He works here, doesn't he? Is he taking on side work or something?"

Her brother stopped walking and turned to face her. "Things are different around here, Sum."

That much was obvious. The falling down sign, the over-grown lawn... "Money troubles?"

"Partly. With Dad and Nana both having health issues, Mom's stretched as thin as can be. Jilly and I help where we can, but we've got businesses to run, too."

Summer gestured to the second barn. "But you're both on

the premises to see what's going on. Like, why is the sign falling down? And the house is missing a shutter."

Gavin nudged a stone with the toe of his shoe. "It's been an uphill battle. Dad's so stubborn. He swears he can take care of this stuff himself, but he can't, and that really ticks him off."

"Gav, his pride can't take precedence over the business. Believe me, I know how much it sucks to admit you need help. This whole situation?" She waved her hands up and down to encompass herself. "I'm forty-one and I had to come crawling back to Mommy and Daddy because people were being mean to me. My pride is packed up in one of those boxes we just put in the storage unit."

He scowled at her. "Death threats aren't just people being mean. Neither is vandalizing your car. Or destroying your career. Don't downplay it."

She swallowed against the sudden lump in her throat. "I have to. If I let it be what it is, I'll curl up into the fetal position and melt."

He reached out and yanked her against his chest for a bear hug. "I'm glad you're home. If anyone can get Dad to listen, it's you."

"I don't know about that." Summer relished the comforting hug, until Gavin slipped his arm upward and caught her in a headlock. She jabbed her finger into his side.

Laughing, they shoved each other away.

"You better find Mom and get to work."

"Yeah. Wish me luck."

Gavin's smile turned to more of a grimace. "I'm afraid you're gonna need it." With that, he headed off to his bakery, Batter Up!, in The Shoppes.

Summer went into the house and found Andi in the kitchen. "Hey, Mom, when do you want to go over the books and whatnot?"

Andi shifted her gaze and smoothed her hands down the front of her jeans. "You just got home. I figured you'd want to start maybe next Monday."

"Today's only Wednesday. I don't need almost a week off. I'll take this stuff up to my room and we can get started." She thought about her brief conversation with Gavin. "If it's a payroll issue, don't worry about getting me set up until Monday. I just need to get busy and keep my mind off things, okay?"

"Alright," Andi sighed. "Let me grab a few things and I'll meet you in the office in an hour?"

"Sounds good." She grabbed a suitcase and a small box and headed up the stairs. She'd gotten halfway up when her mom called after her.

"Summer?"

She stopped and hunkered down to look back. "Yeah?"

"I'm glad you're home."

"Me, too." It was mostly true. She was glad to be home, surrounded by familiar people who loved her and weren't trying to destroy her life. There was also an expiration date on that gladness. Being an adult under her parents' roof wasn't going to be a comforting situation for long. Before the week was out, she'd start looking for an apartment.

Summer walked past Willow Hall, the barn that was original to the property, to get to The Shoppes, which housed the office on the second floor. This barn was built in the nineties, constructed to match the aesthetic of the original barn, but with modern construction and amenities like air conditioning and indoor plumbing.

At first, it was used to host weddings, while the original

barn was renovated and updated. Even though they still called it "the farm," the property hadn't been an actual working farm since the eighties, when the fields were sold off to neighboring farms. The original barn was brought into the twenty-first century with all new electric, plumbing, flooring... the works. When it was done, they'd christened it Willow Hall.

Once that was complete, they renovated and repurposed The Shoppes, which had never been an actual working barn. They divided the main floor into two separate shops with a spacious lobby with display cases and a large counter with seating to serve clients of all three businesses. They'd renamed the building The Shoppes and customized the spaces for Jilly's Blooms and Batter Up!. The second floor now housed the farm's office and a massive storage space filled with tons of tables and chairs and linens.

Lastly, the third "barn" had been built specifically with events in mind, on the opposite side of the property. Unofficially, it was Barn Three. Officially, it was Creekside Hall.

Summer jogged up the stairs and pushed open the door to the office, then came to a dead stop. Stacks of papers and folders overflowed from the desk and chairs. It looked like a paper factory exploded across the tops of the filing cabinets and even the floor. What the heck was going on? Her mom had always kept the office super organized.

She rounded the desk and gaped at the mountains of paper on either side of the plush chair. She was still looking slowly around the room, taking it all in, when Andi came in behind her.

"I know it's a mess..."

Summer heard a sadness in her mother's voice she'd never heard before. She crossed the room and closed the door. Two folding chairs faced the desk. Summer took the files off the chairs and flopped them onto the floor with the others. She sat in one chair and gestured to the other.

"Mom?"

Andi sat slowly. She held a box and settled it on her lap.

"What's going on? This is..." She gestured to the room but couldn't think of a word to describe it.

"I know." Andi sighed and stared down at the box. "I started keeping receipts in the house because things were getting lost in here." Tears welled up in her eyes. She waved around at the room. "Half of this junk is duplicates and triplicates I printed and then printed again because I couldn't find the originals."

"What happened?"

"Everything. With your dad's health, Nana's health, business slowing down, trying to handle everything... I can't do it all like I used to."

For the first time, Summer recognized that her mother wasn't an immortal superwoman. It was sobering, and it also sparked a determination in her. Her mother had always been the rock of the family. Summer couldn't remember a single time she'd ever asked for help. It was time for her mom to get some support.

She reached over and squeezed her mother's hand. "You don't have to do it all. That's why I'm here. I promise, I'll get everything under control."

Her chin quivered as she nodded, still staring down at the box.

"There's nothing wrong with needing help. Or a break."

Andi pulled in a deep breath and let it out, then steeled her shoulders and fixed her gaze on Summer. "I don't know how it got this bad."

"These things snowball into an avalanche so fast, but that doesn't matter. We'll get it sorted out." She looked around the room, taking stock. The biggest issue was loose paper. Lots and lots of loose paper. "I think it looks worse than it is. Let's grab two of the long tables from the storeroom and set them up, then we can get everything up off the ground and start sorting."

They hauled the tables over and spent the afternoon making neat piles. No sorting, just stacking.

While they worked, Summer said, "We should probably make this official. What's my job title?" Her mom hadn't hesitated to give her a job, but there hadn't been time to iron out any details other than the salary.

Andi straightened another stack of paper. "What would you like it to be? Business Manager? Event Planner?"

"What do you plan for me to do? Handle the office and event planning?"

"I'll still work in the office," Andi said, but she didn't sound sure.

"First, you need a break. I don't know what all's going on with Dad and Nana, but it sounds like that's where you need to focus your energy, right?"

"Yeah," she sighed.

"How about Facility Manager and Event Planner?"

"Sounds fancy. I like it." Andi smiled for the first time all afternoon.

Summer stopped working and turned to face her mom. This part of the conversation wasn't going to be easy. "Mom."

"What?" Andi stopped fiddling with papers and gave Summer her attention.

She swallowed hard. "If you want me to help you, you need to let me help you. My expertise is both business management and event planning. I know what I'm doing, so if you want me to work here, you're going to have to let me have the authority to do whatever needs done. Obviously, I fully expect you to be involved and have oversight in your own business. But I'm going to want to change some things and create and streamline procedures, and I'm not willing to be micromanaged. I need you to trust me like you would any manager you'd hire." She already knew her mom was mostly on board. The salary she'd offered was reasonable for the position and the area, so at least her mom recognized she wasn't a teenager working for minimum wage at the family business.

"I know."

"Dad, too."

Andi shook her head. "I have no control over that. I'll do my best to keep him out of your hair, but it's going to be a lot harder for him to get on board. You know that."

"Yeah." Summer opened the box of receipts her mom had brought from the house and leafed through the pile. A four-thousand-dollar slip caught her eye. "What is this?" She held it out for Andi to inspect.

"A refund."

"What? Why?"

Andi sighed again. "It was one of our spring brides. They'd rented Creekside Hall for her reception but it was cold and windy and pouring rain so they couldn't use the patio and they couldn't have the doors up."

"So what?" Summer looked down over the receipt. "Her wedding was April eighteenth. Unpredictable weather is the rule, not the exception. Especially that time of year."

"I know, but when she complained, I felt bad she couldn't do pictures out at the gazebo or on the patio like she wanted."

"Too bad." Summer was confused. Her mom had always been a shrewd businesswoman who never would have refunded the bulk of her reception costs back to a bride just because of the weather. The weather! The worst part was that weather is clearly covered in the contract, so there was absolutely no need to give this greedy bridezilla a penny back.

Andi's shoulders drooped. "To be honest, it was just easier to refund her money and not have to deal with it."

Summer put an arm around her mom's back and hugged her. "I wish you'd have told me you needed help."

"Yeah, right." She chuckled. "That's not exactly part of my vocabulary."

"It should be."

"Look who's talking. How hard was it for you to say you needed to come home?"

"Touché." She tapped the side of the box. "Am I going to find anything else like that in here?"

"Not like that, no."

Another hour later, all of the papers and loose files were stacked neatly on the two long tables, ready to be attacked and sorted. The desk, floor, and tops of the file cabinets were clear.

"I think it's time to call it a day," Summer said.

"Agreed. Supper should be done by now. I made that ranch chicken in the crockpot that you like."

"Awesome."

They walked back into the house and Summer was immediately swept up in big hugs from her dad and grandmother. Her dad positively beamed at her and told her a dozen times how glad he was that she was home.

Even her sister managed to give her a quick hug. "Welcome home, Summer."

"Thanks, Jillian."

The hard business conversation with Dad would have to wait for another day.

Chapter Five

Monday morning, Ben rolled up to Willow Creek with a to do list in mind. He planned to finish the mowing he'd abandoned last Wednesday when Summer came home, then he wanted to do the trimming along the stone fences at the entrance.

Summer walked out of The Shoppes with a clipboard and a look of determination. Her hair was tied up in a long ponytail that swung across her back as she moved.

"Hey, Sum," he said as she headed toward Creekside Hall.

She startled, then turned and made a beeline for him. "Just who I wanted to see."

"Uh oh, should I run?" He was only half-joking. She looked intense.

A wicked grin turned the corners of her mouth upward. "You can run if you want to, but if memory serves, I'm faster than you."

"Maybe twenty years ago."

She rolled her eyes. "Anyway. I wanted to get your take on what's going on around here."

He immediately went on high alert. He didn't want to get

enmeshed in some family drama. He might be an honorary part of the family, but there were still some boundaries. "What do you mean?" he asked carefully.

She stared at him for a long moment, then said, "Walk with me."

They walked to the end of the driveway, where the big wooden "Welcome to Willow Creek" sign dangled from a single corner chain. Summer flicked the broken chain that had a good amount of rust.

"For starters, I mean this."

He reached up and scratched the back of his neck. "Um, yeah, I don't know."

"Ben."

"Summer."

"I'm serious. Things are not right. The office is a hot mess, Mom looks like she's one burnt piece of toast away from a nuclear meltdown, and everywhere I look, there's something that needs fixed. I thought that was your job, but Gavin said you're working elsewhere, too. Ben, please."

The concern in her voice was loud and clear. And justified. Ben knew things were slipping around the farm, but again, he didn't feel like it was his place to do anything more than offer to help wherever they needed him to. On the other hand, this was Summer, and he felt like he owed it to her to tell her what he knew.

"Every time I talked to Mom or Dad or Nana from Chicago, all they told me is that business is great, everything's great." She blinked rapidly and hugged the clipboard to her chest. "I went online this morning and looked at our reviews. The last time I looked, we had a solid five star rating everywhere."

He grimaced and leaned back as if he could protect himself from her words. "What is it now?"

"Three." She held up three fingers to illustrate the point. "Help me. I can't fix this if I don't know everything."

He looked past her, up the driveway, to the big white farmhouse where he'd spent most of his childhood. Being Gavin's best friend meant he was part of the family. Andi and Mack treated him exactly the same as their own kids. Up to and including being grabbed by the ear and parked in the corner of the kitchen by Andi when he'd thought – once – that he could talk back to her because she wasn't his mom. Boy, had he been mistaken.

In some ways, it wasn't his concern. But in other, very real and important ways, it was.

He began with, "I don't want to point any fingers or lay the blame at any one person's feet. Everyone could probably do a lot of things differently or better or whatever, myself included."

Summer heaved an annoyed sigh. "Great. Blah, blah, blah, I acknowledge your legal disclaimer." She rolled her hand to hurry him along.

"It kind of started going downhill probably six years ago with your dad's heart attack."

"His *what*?!" Summer dropped the clipboard. Her eyes bugged and her mouth flopped as she tried to make words come out.

Crap. He had no idea she didn't know about that. Why would they keep that from her? Oh, boy.

He bent down and picked up the clipboard and the pen that had rolled several feet away. "Sorry. I assumed you knew."

Her lips pursed and tears spilled down her cheeks. He'd seen that expression many, many times over the years. Those weren't sad tears. She was livid.

"Obviously he's okay now. It was mild. I don't think he was

in the hospital more than two days. I'm sure they didn't want to worry you." The words sounded lame to his own ears. She was right to be angry. He knew she hated it when her angry tears got attention, so he ignored them and kept talking. "Anyway. Your dad was told to take it easy, and you know how stubborn he can be. He started doing even more just to prove he could, but he'd get tired out pretty fast and so I'd follow behind him trying to wrap up all these unfinished projects he'd start."

Summer swiped the tears from her cheeks.

"Your mom was trying to rein him in, and then—Please tell me you know Nana fell and broke her hip." That had happened a little more than four years ago.

She nodded.

He nervously clicked the pen a few times until Summer grabbed it from him. He never intended to tell anyone this next part, but he felt like he should tell Summer. "One of my paychecks bounced."

"Noooo, that can't be." Her eyes were huge.

He held up a hand and quickly went on. "Your mom made it right immediately. She was so upset. Something about she had forgotten to transfer or deposit money into the payroll account. I get it. There was so much going on. Then your dad decided to hire a new maintenance guy. I found out one Monday morning when he showed up and I was supposed to show him around." That was the part that bothered him the most.

"Wait, weren't you doing the maintenance?"

"Yeah. After the check incident, your dad got it in his head that I was going to quit and leave them high and dry so... well, basically I was just part time after that." Essentially, Mack had left *him* high and dry, so he'd had to scramble and turn his side jobs into his main job. He wasn't bitter or angry anymore, but it had been a good lesson to look out for himself.

"I had no idea."

"It worked out okay. I started my own business, and when the other guy didn't work out, your mom begged me to come back. I compromised and took them on as a client. Now I'm just here off and on doing odd jobs."

She looked skeptical. "And going around doing odd jobs supports you?"

For some reason, he didn't tell her his business was booming. He was able to come here and help out exactly because in four years, he'd built a full roster of talented, trusted employees who handled the big jobs. His position had evolved to where he was a lot more hands-off, inspecting his employees' work when necessary, and honestly, picking and choosing what he wanted to do personally. Or not do. Perks of being the owner. "Yeah, I support myself doing odd jobs." Maybe not as well as her celebrity chef ex-boyfriend, but very comfortably.

"Would odd jobs include fixing this sign?" She tilted her head at smiled up at him.

He eyed the sign with a little trepidation. "Your dad says it's on his list." Truth be told, he'd wanted to fix it ever since it broke during a brutal February ice storm. Seven months ago. But Mack had insisted he was going to get to it. No amount of cajoling or nagging on Andi's part had made him move any faster.

She sighed and scratched her head. "I don't get it. I was home not even a year ago and I didn't see any of this."

"The sign didn't break until this past winter, and I'm guessing you didn't spend much time in the barns when you were visiting."

"I suppose." She pushed the dangling corner of the heavy sign and it spun in a slow circle. "This is just bad for business.

If this is someone's first impression, there's no way they're going to trust us with their important event."

Ben didn't want to step into the middle of what was certain to become family drama, but she was right. He stepped over to the sign and took a good look. The wood was split in a couple places, and the paint on the plaque itself was chipped and peeling. Apparently he was going to jump right in it, because he found himself saying, "I'll fix the chain now before I mow. I'll see about getting the frame and the plaque fixed in the next week or so."

"Promise?" Summer held out her pinkie.

Ben wrapped his pinkie around hers. "Promise." A pinkie promise was as good as a blood oath around here. "But no guarantees as to how long it'll hold."

"You're the best."

"Your dad's not going to be happy."

Summer's lip quirked into a wry smile. She tapped the clipboard. "He might not even notice once he sees *my* list." A second later, she said, "I might need your help with this, too. I'm just going to make a list of the things I see, but maybe if you have time you can walk around with me and let me know if there are other things that need repair, like electrical or whatever?"

A chance to spend time with Summer? So maybe she'd start to see him as an actual man and not a "bonus" little brother or Gavin's friend? Yeah, he'd take that opportunity any day of the week. His answer was casual. "Yeah, sure."

"Probably towards the end of the week? I'm trying to organize the office, which is going to take forever."

"Sure. I'll get your chain fixed for now."

They started walking back up the driveway. She cut to the right, to Creekside Hall, and he went left to the shed.

"Thanks, Ben."

"No problem." Even as he said it, he was pretty sure there were going to be a lot of problems now that Summer was back home. For instance, he'd had himself convinced Summer was a blip in his past, but the flutter in his chest when he was near her suggested otherwise.

No problem? Yeah, right.

Chapter Six

Summer walked through the "new" building that was six years old at this point. Creekside Hall itself was a sort of industrial building, but the brown siding and black trim and wide roll-up doors fit in with the rustic farm surroundings.

Inside, the grand ballroom boasted rough-hewn wood beams across the ceiling with strings of dimmable Edison-style lightbulbs with a visible glowing filament that gave off a romantic glow.

She flicked the light switch and sucked in an annoyed breath. A full quarter of the bulbs were burned out. She snapped a picture with her phone so she could note exactly which ones needed replaced. At least the stained concrete floor still looked brand new.

Next, she went to the hidden control panel and hit the buttons to raise each of the eight roll-up doors. Seven of them rolled up. Six of them rolled back down when she hit the button again.

The list on her clipboard stretched longer every time she turned a corner or flipped a switch.

She peeked into the storage room and made another note to check all the tables, chairs, and linens. That was a project for another day. Everything looked okay in the dressing room and the restrooms. She even flushed both toilets and checked the sink faucets. For once, the things she touched functioned like they were supposed to.

"You need a hand?"

Ben's voice from the small lobby caught her attention. "No, I think I'm good."

He pointed toward the ballroom. "The door's up. I figured you couldn't get it to come down."

"Oh. Yeah, that. I hit the button but nothing."

From the way he nodded, it was clear he already knew it wasn't working. "There's something wrong with the connection."

"Let me guess. It's on Dad's list?"

His silence was an answer. He cleared his throat and said, "I'll show you how to put it down manually."

He went into the storage room and came back with a hook on a long handle.

Summer took it from him. "Tell me what to do so when you're not here I'll know how to do it." She followed his direction to catch the hook onto a groove on the door and pulled it down to where she could reach. From there, she pulled the door all the way down and Ben showed her where the hidden lever was to lock it in place. "Thanks."

"No problem." He jerked his thumb toward the outside. "I got the sign rehung, but the wood's in pretty bad shape so I don't know if it'll last until I can get a new one made."

"Hopefully it does. If not, we're just back where we started, right?" She looked up at the ceiling. "Hey, do you happen to know if we have more of these lightbulbs anywhere?"

"There might be a handful in the storage room behind the office, but not enough to replace all of the ones that are out."

It didn't take long for her to see a pattern. Ben knew it needed fixed, but Dad insisted he was going to take care of it, so Ben felt his hands were tied. And now here they were, with a million little things that had grown from a molehill into a mountain.

"Guess I need to order bulbs when I get back to the office."

Ben made a noise.

"What?"

"You might want to check with your dad. He keeps telling me he has a guy."

She rolled her eyes. "A lightbulb guy."

"Yeah."

"Oh, for Pete's sake." She was not looking forward to the big meeting she had to have with both her parents as soon as she got all these broken ducks in a row. In the handful of days since she'd gotten home, he'd changed the subject every time the business came up, waving it away as something to be discussed later. Unfortunately for both of them, later was here.

"Good luck," Ben said with a laugh as he headed for the door.

At least Ben seemed to be in her corner. She had a feeling she was going to be fighting an uphill battle with her dad. Mom and Gavin would likely straddle the fence and try to keep the peace, and Jillian would definitely side with Dad, no matter what. Nana was a wild card.

Summer followed Ben out and watched him hop back on the riding mower. As her mind turned over the idea of the meeting, Ben's movement caught her attention. He slung his leg over the tractor and started it. He looked pretty darn good in his jeans and a plain gray t-shirt that skimmed his tight abs.

Even his baseball cap—. She stopped herself and smacked her forehead with the clipboard. Where had *that* come from? It had to be because he was the polar opposite of super suave, polished, and fake Michael Mastriano. He was *Ben*, for Pete's sake. Clearly she needed to focus on work.

She hustled back to the office. She'd make her list for Willow Hall later.

The lobby of The Shoppes smelled like flowers and cake, a combination that could sometimes be overpowering, but right now it was perfectly balanced. The door to Jillian's flower shop stood open. For a second, she debated going in and talking to her sister, but decided against it. There'd be time for that drama later.

Upstairs in the office, she sat at the desk, hands perched in midair, not sure what to tackle first. No wonder her mother had gotten overwhelmed.

She leaned back in the office chair and had a mini-heart attack as it reared back like a bull about to buck her off. She grabbed the edge of the desk and sat forward, then snatched a pencil and scrawled "NEW CHAIR" on her ridiculously long list of things that needed to be addressed.

Over the weekend, she'd organized papers into piles of bills, receipts, and contracts. Another stack held important miscellaneous things that needed addressed. Three boxes sat stacked beside the door, full of duplicate papers that needed to be shredded. That was a project for a later date. A much, much later date.

The office door burst open.

"What's the big idea?" her dad demanded.

Summer gasped in surprise. It took a second to make sense of the sudden intrusion. "What?"

Andi was two steps behind. "Mack, what are you doing?"

He crossed his arms and scowled. "We come back from town and as we pull in I see the sign."

Summer gave her head a little shake. "Are you seriously mad the sign is hanging like it's supposed to?"

His brows pinched inward. "No, that's not it."

Andi huffed out a humorless laugh.

"I have things I'm going to do," he said. "I can take care of it. I don't need you coming in here and putting your nose where it doesn't need to be."

Summer started to lean back in the chair, but the wobble reminded her it was unstable, so she changed course and leaned forward, putting her elbows on the desk. "Dad, there are a lot of things that need done. The sign was just one quick job and now you can take it off your list."

"I don't need you telling me what to take off my list."

"Where is this list? We can prioritize what needs done."

He tapped his temple. "It's all up here."

"It needs to be on here." She slid a notebook across the desk.

His eyes widened and the vein in his neck throbbed. "You think you're going to tell me how things need done? Listen here—"

Andi put a hand on his arm. "Mack, stop."

"No, you stop."

"Don't you take that tone with me," Andi snapped.

He shot her a look, but backed down.

Summer felt herself regressing back to childhood. Her dad had a big personality and a particular affection for being right. A lot of times he was, so it wasn't an issue often. But when it was an issue, it was an *issue*. And yeah, this was shaping up to be one of those times.

Andi planted her hands on her hips. "Summer is here to

run the business. That means she's making decisions and getting things done, whether you like it or not."

Mack pointed at her. "That is *not* how this is going to go."

Andi's cheeks reddened. She bit out, "If you'd like to keep that finger attached to your hand, I suggest getting it out of my face."

He yanked his hand back.

"Summer's job is facility manager."

"No. She's just here to plan weddings."

Andi sucked in an annoyed breath. "No. That's what you thought she was coming back to do, and I told you a thousand times she's not just planning parties."

"Well, she can manage this," he said, waving at the office, "and leave my stuff alone."

"That's not how this works."

Summer watched the exchange and wanted to melt into the floor. She wondered if Reesa had only tanked her reputation in Chicago. Maybe she could get a job in New York or Dallas. Juneau?

"She's not coming in here and telling me what to do!" her dad roared.

How about Tokyo? That *might* be far enough away.

"Stop yelling!" Andi shouted back.

Nope, maybe Sydney. Were they still planning to take tour groups to the moon? She pressed her fingers to her temples. This was so bizarre. Her parents never used to yell at each other.

"Please stop," Summer pleaded.

They quieted. Her dad scowled at the far wall while her mom looked like she was fighting tears.

Summer's throat tightened. Things were so much worse than she thought. She tried to be sympathetic to her dad's position. He probably felt like he was being pushed out and overwhelmed by the things that needed done. And no doubt he felt like he should be able to handle it all.

But she was really worried about her mom. If something didn't change fast, they were all going to find out what happens when the person who handles everything finally gets crushed under the weight of all that responsibility.

Chapter Seven

"How are you doing with Summer being back home?" Gavin asked around a mouthful of his burger.

As they did almost every week, Ben and Gavin sat in a booth at Rosie's Diner, a tiny dive restaurant with delicious, hearty, cheap food at the edge of town. Ben speared a piece of grilled chicken from his salad. "Fine, why?"

"Hey, you're talking to *me* here."

Ben stabbed at a wedge of cucumber. "It's fine. Really. A bit weird, but it's okay."

"You still…" he trailed off, waving his finger in a circle to encompass the past.

"I haven't even seen her in eight years, Gav." Because he avoided the farm like the plague every time she came home.

Gavin was unconvinced.

"No. I'm over her." He didn't exactly *regret* having a few too many beers a couple of years ago and blurting out "I would have told Summer I loved her" when they were talking about things they'd do over if they could, but he did wish it was something Gavin would forget.

"No offense, but I'm not buying it. I see the way you look at her."

That was okay. Ben didn't buy it himself. Having Summer back home, back in his life, made him realize his feelings hadn't faded as much as he would have liked. "Makes no difference.' I don't think she'll ever see me as anything other than her annoying kid brother's best friend." He drew a long sip of soda and redirected the topic. "I'm more interested in how she's dealing with being back. Big changes."

Gavin blew out a puff of air. "You're not kidding. I don't think I even realized how bad things have gotten until I started looking with fresh eyes. It happens so gradually, you know? It's one little thing, then ten little things, and all of a sudden, it's a whole big thing. It's a good thing she's come back so we can get it back up to snuff, but she's got some pretty big obstacles in her way."

"Your dad?"

Gavin nodded. "He doesn't like it when things change or when he's not in control. I try to stay out of his way, so I know she's got an uphill battle."

"It's not just her battle, you know. If Willow Creek goes under..." he trailed off, letting the words hang in the air between them. Ben knew his best friend didn't like conflict, especially with his family, but it couldn't only be on Summer's shoulders to handle their dad, fix the business, and deal with the ongoing fallout from her very public breakup with that idiot chef guy.

Gavin sat back in the booth and eyed him for a long moment. "You're right. I'll put on my big boy pants and make sure I've got her back. I guess I never allowed myself to think it was a possibility that the farm could ever be in so much trouble we can't come back from it. But we're there, aren't we?"

Ben shrugged. He hadn't intended to go into a deep discussion, but that's where they'd landed. "I don't think it's anywhere near the point of no return." He took another bite of salad. This shouldn't be any of his business, but he'd been so close for so long that Willow Creek was a part of him almost as much as it was a part of Gavin.

"Good deflection, by the way." Gavin's eye sparkled. "So if you're not still waiting around for Summer, have you been seeing anyone?"

Ben waved a hand. "Too busy."

"Bull."

"You're one to talk. You haven't dated anyone since She Who Will Not Be Named."

"Still traumatized."

They laughed at that, but Ben knew there was a fair amount of truth to it. Gavin's last serious girlfriend had turned out to be an awful person who showed her true colors when she demanded Gavin choose between her and his family because she felt he was spending too much time helping with Nana's care while her broken hip healed.

"How's your mom?" Gavin asked.

"Much better. She still gets worn out really fast, but otherwise she's good." A few months earlier, Susie ended up with a nasty case of pneumonia that landed her in the hospital for three days. It would have been longer, but she demanded to be released so she could go home and get some actual rest.

"Maybe I'll pop over and see her."

"You need a guinea pig, I take it?" Ben's mom, a blue-ribbon winning home baker, was Gavin's go-to flavor tester.

"New blueberry lemon recipe. I think it's better than my old one, but your mom'll be a better judge of that."

"Oooh, it better be good. You know how much she loves your blueberry lemon cake as it is."

"I know. This one has a bit more citrus, so I think she'll approve."

They ate in silence for a few minutes before Gavin said, "I saw Toby Duggan the other day. He was really happy with whatever you guys did for him. Said Mike was great. Apparently even his dog liked him and his dog doesn't like anybody."

Ben grinned. "Glad to hear it. We reinforced a wall in his basement."

"Yeah, that's what it was. Something about termites or something."

"Yup." Ben pushed his empty salad bowl away. "Hey, do you ever ship cakes?"

"There are a few I'm willing to ship. Some are just sturdier for shipping. Why?"

"Taylor and Kyler's birthdays are coming up. I thought it might be fun to send them a cake. A little more personal than gift cards." His niece and nephew lived in Florida. Their birthdays were three years and two days apart.

Gavin sat back and thought a minute. "We can definitely do something. Maybe a half and half cake."

"What's that?"

Gavin pulled a pen out of his shirt pocket and sketched a circle on a napkin. "Just like it sounds. This half could be chocolate and this half vanilla. Or if they like the same flavor cake I can do the icing half and half." He drew some lines. "I could do an arced 'Happy Birthday' this way, then put her name here and his name here."

Ben watched the design unfold and found himself impressed with Gavin's creativity. "That's incredible. Can you do a marble cake?"

Gavin shot him a mock offended look. "In my sleep."

"Okay, okay, it was a dumb question. I meant is a marble cake one you can ship?"

Gavin chuckled at him. "Yes. But I warn you, it's not cheap, and there's nothing I can do about shipping rates."

"Nothing's cheap these days."

"You're not kidding." He sobered. "Which is why fixing all this stuff at the farm at one time is going to hurt a lot worse than doing it as it needs done. I really should have paid more attention."

"Hey, it's hard to argue with your parents when they say they've got everything under control. Mine are the same way. They *want* to take care of everything the way they always have, but it's not as easy as it was five or ten years ago."

"That's for sure. And you know how Dad is. If he says he's gonna do something, he gets testy if someone else goes ahead and does it. Like it's some kind of weakness to say he can't do it all himself."

Ben tipped back his cup and took the last swallow of soda.

Gavin did the same, then said, "Well, I guess I'll go back to the farm and see if there's anything I can do for Summer. Can't have big sis taking all the heat all the time."

Ben agreed. He was fully prepared to go to bat for Summer any way he could.

Chapter Eight

Summer grabbed the laptop and her list. She decided to go catalogue the issues in Willow Hall and leave her parents to argue without her.

She pushed through the doors and pulled in a deep breath. Fall was making its presence known, with the threat of a chill hiding behind the warm day. Every time the sun ducked behind a cloud, the temperature dropped fast. Summer hurried across the parking lot, making a mental note that at least the asphalt parking lot that connected Willow Hall and The Shoppes was in great shape. It would probably need a new sealcoat in two or three years, but for now, it was one of the few things she could completely ignore.

By now, the only truly original part of the former barn was the stone foundation. The building itself had been fixed and updated and remodeled many times over the years, until its current iteration. The outside was deep red, with siding that looked like wood, but up close you could see it was actually a composite material that would outlast any of the Sullivans and it never needed painted.

The doors and windows were trimmed in a deep brown

that was almost black, a striking accent to the red. She breathed a sigh of relief. At least the structures were in great shape, so the updates and fixes should mostly be cosmetic.

Her optimism tanked as soon as she walked in the front door. There were... *things*... everywhere. Tables that belonged in storage, boxes, stacks of haphazardly folded linens, piles of not-even-sort-of folded linens, and more boxes. Apparently it had been this way for a while, because a layer of dust covered everything. Cobwebs pre-decorated the windows for Halloween.

Summer had no idea how long she stood in the doorway, taking in the depressing atmosphere. She reached over and flipped the light switch. There was a slight sizzling noise that probably wasn't great. She opened the laptop and started a new document so she could list what needed to be addressed. Then she realized it would be too cumbersome to carry around, so she set it on the nearest table, on top of a pile of linens. A puff of dust rose from the fabric. The top linen featured a yellow crusty splotch that had probably been an expensive sauce at some point and could have been laundered out at that point, but no more.

She made a note to check when the last event had been held in this building. In fact, she scratched a note to look over the events for the last few years so she could track the obvious decline. Judging from the crusted linens and dust, there hadn't been an event in this building for a good six months. Why not? Was it a matter of this becoming the dumping ground so nothing was scheduled for this building? She hoped that was the case, because it was an easy enough fix.

Oh, well. Might as well make the most of the situation. She plugged her phone into the sound system and let the music help her focus. With the clipboard and pen in hand, she worked counter-clockwise around the room. She was in the far corner, flipping to a fresh sheet of paper, swaying to a catchy song when Ben shouted.

"Summer, you're on fire!"

She grinned as she wrote a note to hire a cleaning service. She hadn't heard him come in. "Yeah, I'm making some real progress."

"No, *fire*."

She spun around to see Ben whacking at the pile of smoking linens. The clipboard clattered to the ground as she lurched forward and raced across the room.

Sparks flashed out the side of the laptop and a tiny flame made an appearance in the middle of the keyboard, melting the letter H.

Summer grabbed the fire extinguisher. "Move!" She pointed the black hose at the smoldering mess and squeezed the trigger as soon as Ben jumped out of the way.

A puff of white powder wheezed out of the nozzle.

She looked down at the extinguisher. The gauge's needle pointed to red. Empty.

Ben grabbed the smoking pile and ran for the door.

Summer dropped the useless extinguisher and ran after him.

He hurled the armful onto the asphalt.

The laptop skidded across the parking lot, a few pieces breaking off and landing several feet away.

They stamped on the linens until the last of the smoke dissipated.

Summer looked over to thank Ben, but noticed the angry red welt on his forearm. She rushed over and grabbed his hand, pulling his arm out so she could see better. "Ben, you're hurt."

He looked down and winced. "Didn't even feel it until you said that."

"Adrenaline."

"Let's make sure nothing else is smoldering."

Summer followed him back inside. Everything was normal except for the new scorch mark on the table and the faint smell of smoke hanging in the air.

"You okay?" he asked.

"Yeah, just a little freaked out. If you hadn't come in..." She shuddered. "And a whole lot mad." She nudged the useless fire extinguisher with the toe of her shoe. "This is unacceptable."

"Agreed." Ben grimaced.

"Let's go in the house and take care of that arm."

"It's fine."

"It's not fine, and I'm not taking no for an answer."

He flashed a lopsided smile. "You're cute when you're bossy."

She couldn't think of a comeback, which seemed to amuse him even more.

Chapter Nine

Ben double checked that the linens were nowhere near an outlet, even though he was pretty sure the fire had started from the laptop. The mark on his arm stung and began to throb.

Summer went out the door ahead of him. "I can clean this up after we get your arm taken care of."

He didn't argue, and didn't mention that he wasn't going to leave it for her to clean up herself. They walked to the house and she parked him at the kitchen table while she got the first aid kit from the powder room. She set the plastic case on the table and popped it open.

His arm did hurt, but it wasn't nearly as bad as he'd first thought. An angry red welt, about an inch wide and maybe four inches long, stood out on his inner forearm. He was glad he'd taken the brunt of it and that Summer hadn't been hurt.

Summer unscrewed the cap from a tube of burn cream. "Do you think we should go to the ER?"

He propped his arm on the table and clenched his teeth as she spread the cream on the injury. It hurt more now than it had a few minutes ago. "No. There aren't even any blisters, so there's no sense dropping money for an ER copay or taking a spot from someone with a real emergency."

She was quiet as she applied the cream.

"You okay?"

Her gaze darted up to meet his, surprised. "Me? I'm fine. You're the one who got burned." She blinked a few times. "I'm really sorry you got hurt."

"Hey. It's no big deal." He was just glad he'd gotten there before the fire turned dangerous. That pile of tablecloths could easily have gone up in real flames, and the amount of smoke they would have produced could have quickly overwhelmed Summer. The could haves swirled through his mind faster than he could push them away.

"It is." She shoved the lid back on the cream and screwed the top on with force. The tube twisted and she threw it back in the case. "It's all my fault. I didn't even see it, and I never should have left the laptop there. If you hadn't come in…"

"Summer. Look at me."

Reluctantly, she turned and her blue eyes met his.

"I'm fine. You're fine. It's just a few dirty tablecloths and a crappy old laptop. No. Big. Deal."

"It is, though. The fire extinguisher. Why wasn't it charged?"

He couldn't argue with her there. "That's a separate issue. I'm okay. This—" he held up the arm she'd just bandaged "—is truly no big deal. It doesn't even hurt."

Okay, that bit was a little white lie, because it did hurt. A lot, actually. But she didn't need to know that.

She chewed on her bottom lip as she closed the first aid kit. He knew her mind must be racing even more than it had been.

"Let's go clean up the mess, okay?"

She crossed her arms. "You do *not* have to help. It's my fault, my mess, and I'll take care of it."

Ben stood and put his hands on her shoulders. "Summer. It's not your fault. It's not your mess, and you don't have to fix everything yourself."

"Thanks, Ben, but I've got everything under control."

He didn't mean to laugh, but he did.

"Wow." She stepped back, out of his reach.

There was nothing he could say to make the faux pas go away, so he just mumbled, "Sorry."

She took the first aid kit back to the powder room.

He followed her out the front door, back to Willow Hall. She didn't stop him, but she kept speeding up until they were all-out sprinting back to the pile of burned linens.

"Feel better?" he asked as they bent to pick up the tablecloths.

"I don't know what I feel." She sighed and jabbed her finger in the direction of the laptop. "I had all my lists on there. Everything all nice and organized in color-coded spreadsheets. And now it's gone. I threw all my notes away." Her shoulders slumped. "I'm going to have to start from scratch."

"When did you throw them away?"

"Yesterday." She huffed a humorless laugh. "Good timing, wasn't it?"

He said, "Trash doesn't go until tomorrow."

"Yeah, but it's already in the dumpster."

"We're headed there anyway," he said, shaking the armload of linens for emphasis.

"I'm not climbing in the dumpster."

"Come on, it'll be fun. I'll dangle you in by your ankles."

"You're hilarious," she said sarcastically.

"I promise I won't drop you."

"Benjamin. I am not climbing in the dumpster." She was clearly not amused.

"Seriously, it's probably right on top."

She eyed him skeptically.

They rounded the barn and walked over to the big green dumpster. Ben shifted his load to free his left arm and lifted the black lid that covered half of the dumpster. In a testament to the slow business, the container was only about a quarter-full. Before he could throw the linens away, a pair of beady eyes met his. He jumped backward, dropping the cloths on the ground. The lid banged shut.

"What was that?" Summer asked, concerned.

"Raccoon."

"Oh, crap."

"Back up." He moved to the opposite edge of the dumpster and lifted the left lid, flinging it hard so it flipped all the way open. From the far corner under the right side, the eyes regarded him cautiously. Then, a second, smaller, pair of eyes glinted in the darkness. "Shoot, there's at least two of them."

"How'd they get in there?"

"I'm more concerned with how they're getting out."

Before he could come up with a solution, Summer set the laptop on the ground. "I'll get the ladder. You keep an eye on our new friends."

"Sure." The raccoons were still, probably waiting to see whether they'd need to eat his face or not.

Several long minutes later, Summer came back, riding the tractor, hauling two ladders in the dumpcart behind her. "I figured we could set one on the outside and one on the inside so they can get out themselves.

"Good idea." Ben grabbed one of the ladders and carefully eased it down into the dumpster, trying not to disturb the hill of trash. Or the raccoons. The leg of the ladder caught one of the trash bags. It rolled toward the raccoons. The big one – holy cow was it big – lunged forward.

Ben jumped back, his arms cartwheeling to keep his

balance. The back of his heel caught on the separation between the blacktop and the grass, knocking him off-balance. The next thing he knew, he was on his butt in the grass and Summer was laughing.

"I'm sorry," she managed through her laughter.

"You don't look very sorry," he teased as he got to his feet.

"You should have seen your face." She mimicked him, opening her eyes and mouth wide and flailing her arms around.

"The thing jumped right at me. It had to be this big." He held his hands like he was holding an invisible beach ball.

Summer leaned the other ladder on the outside of the dumpster, then backed away quickly and walked over to the grass beside him, still chuckling. "And now we wait."

Luckily, they didn't have to wait long.

A tiny raccoon, about the size of a squirrel, poked its snout up and looked around before scurrying across the edge of the dumpster and leaping to the ground.

Ben looked over at Summer. Her lips were clamped together and her shoulders shook with laughter.

"That is *not* the one that came at me."

She guffawed and grabbed her middle, bending with laughter. "Oh no, it's gonna get me," she mocked. "It's coming right for me."

He just sighed and shook his head. At least she was feeling better, even if it was at his expense. Watching her, he couldn't help but start laughing himself. It was pretty funny that the first raccoon out was about a quarter the size of the one who'd hissed at him.

A minute later, the big raccoon appeared over the rim of the dumpster and jumped down. It quickly waddled toward the weeds near the creek.

"See? I told you it was big."

They waited a few minutes longer just in case there were any stragglers lagging behind the first two.

"I'll see if there are any more." She smirked. "Stay behind me. I'll protect you."

"Keep it up and I *will* dangle you in the dumpster."

"In your dreams," she fired back. She walked over to the dumpcart and held up a grabber pole. "I also brought this. Just in case the bag from my office is near the top." She squeezed the trigger a few times to click the pincher end open and shut.

"Genius."

She peered over the edge and pointed to a bag. "I think it's that one."

Ben leaned over the side of the dumpster.

Summer grabbed his side. "Raccoon!"

He jumped back and dropped the pole. Summer doubled over, laughing so hard tears streamed from her eyes.

Ben crossed his arms. "Do you want help or not?"

"Sorry," she snerked, barely controlling the laughter.

He used the pincher of the grabber pole and snagged the bag to haul it up.

Once she got herself together, she grabbed the bag and declared, "Not it."

There in the parking lot, they sorted through half a dozen bags until Summer gave a relieved grunt. "Finally." She held out a stack of crumpled papers. "I'll just take the whole bag back in and go through it. Hopefully I can reconstruct all my spreadsheets."

"Good thing your papers aren't in the same bag as the kitchen trash."

"You aren't kidding."

They threw the ruined linens in.

"Are you sure you want to toss the laptop? They might be able to get some of the data off it."

She held it up, skeptical. "From this?"

The keyboard was a wavy mess of melted keys. A spiderweb of cracks covered the screen.

"I mean, it's possible the hard drive didn't get damaged. I'll have my guy take a look at it. If not, he can get it recycled." He took the laptop from her and tried to close it, but the hinges were stuck.

"If you really want to, I guess knock yourself out." She shook her head. "But I don't see the point."

He saw the point clearly. Summer was here trying to save everyone around her. If there was anything to salvage on the laptop, he'd be the hero and save her day.

Chapter Ten

The afternoon was a slog of smoothing crumpled papers and lists and recreating spreadsheets in Excel 95 on her mom's ancient desktop computer. It was slow, but it worked well enough. For now.

Summer added "COMPUTER" to her list of things they needed to get, and "FIRE EXTINGUISHER" to the list of things she needed to talk to her dad about.

She heaved out a massive sigh. That was not going to be fun.

She connected to the internet, which took a painfully long time. So long, in fact, that she half expected to hear the *screeeeeeeeeeeeeewoooooooboingboing* from the early days of the internet. When it finally connected, she emailed herself the spreadsheets she'd created. Tomorrow, she'd use her personal laptop since there was no way the company could afford a brand new one right now, but there was no way she was dealing with this one again.

Her phone pinged with a message. It was her mom letting her know dinner was ready. She frowned a little as she checked the time. After six already? *Time really does fly when you're having fun.*

A rumble in her stomach spurred her to get up and flip the light off. The office would still be a mess in the morning and she'd deal with it then.

She hurried down the stairs and nearly ran into Jillian coming out of her shop. "Hey."

"Hey." Her sister was her polar opposite, in disposition as well as physical characteristics. The only thing they shared were blue eyes. Otherwise, Jillian was fair where Summer was dark, Jillian was taller than average while Summer was on the short side. Jillian was quiet and shy, where Summer was outgoing and social. Instead of being each other's yin and yang, though, they were oil and water. Or fire and ice, with Jillian being the ice.

Since she'd been home, she and Jillian had mostly been avoiding each other. She knew Jillian didn't agree with Summer coming in and usurping their dad's way of doing things. And if he was grumbling behind the scenes, it stood to reason that Jillian would take his side and be angry on his behalf without question.

"Smells good. Did you get a new shipment of roses?"

Jillian shook her head. "Gardenias."

"Oh." Summer floundered for something else to say as they crossed the lawn that seemed a lot wider than it had earlier. "I thought those were more like bushes. Like they wouldn't work in bouquets and stuff?"

"They're for topiaries."

Summer had to say something to keep from being trapped in a weird silence with her sister. "Nice. One of the last brides I worked with did miniature rose topiaries as her table settings."

"I'm sure that was lovely."

"It was." Summer gave in to the awkward silence until they

finally reached the house. She was glad when the kitchen was full.

"Just in time, girls," Andi said with a big smile.

As soon as they sat down, on either side of Nana, Nana grabbed their hands. "Gavin, say grace."

Gavin mumbled a short grace. "Amen" was like a gunshot to start a race. Everyone dug into the food in front of them, spooning green beans and roast beef and mashed potatoes onto their plates.

"It's nice to see you girls come in together. Do you have a project you're working on?"

Summer narrowed her eyes. Nana knew better than that.

Jillian said, "No. We just came in at the same time."

Nana didn't say more, but Summer knew she wanted to. It was her personal mission to get them to get along – no, more than get along. She wanted them to be the very best of closest friends and had ever since they were little, but it hadn't happened then, and it definitely wasn't going to happen now.

Gavin said, "Did you get all the gardenias in the fridge, Jilly?"

She immediately softened. Somehow, Gavin was the best brother ever to both Summer and Jillian. "I still have one crate to put away but I think it can wait until morning. I just want to go home and put my feet up."

"I'll put them away for you after dinner. I'm going back out to check my cakes anyway."

"Thanks." She gave him a warm smile.

Andi said, "What cakes are you working on?"

"Birthday cakes for twins turning six. Boy and a girl. The kids picked a castle with a dragon. Challenging, since the parents insisted on no fondant, but I'm having a blast with this one."

Nana scrunched up her face. "I don't like fondant. It tastes like plastic."

"But it looks good. You can do so much with it," Jillian said.

Summer kept her mouth shut. She didn't like the stuff either, but it wasn't worth crossing her sister about.

"Guess we better address the elephant in the room," Mack said. He pushed his plate toward the center of the table and crossed his arms.

"What elephant is that?" Andi asked.

"This is a family business, so the whole family should be involved in any decision making."

Summer looked back and forth between her parents. Clearly her mother had no idea what was coming.

"The family needs to be clear on what everyone's position is."

Andi set her fork down on the table. "We are absolutely not doing this at dinner."

Jillian looked confused. Gavin and Nana wore twin expressions of suspicion. Summer had no idea what her own face reflected, because all she wanted to do was run and hide.

Mack said, "No one was informed about the plan to have Summer come back here and take over and run things."

Andi's mouth pinched and her eyes narrowed. "Just because you can't be bothered to *listen* doesn't mean you weren't told."

Summer wished she hadn't eaten. Her clenched stomach summersaulted in her gut, souring the food. "I'm not trying to take over."

Jillian snorted.

Summer ignored her. "I'm just trying to help."

"Help?" Jillian scoffed. "Everything was more peaceful before you got here."

Andi said, "Things haven't been peaceful around here for

a long time." She cast a meaningful look at Mack, then back at Jillian. "Your dad's right about one thing. We should have had a family meeting a long time ago, because things aren't good."

Jillian reached over and squeezed Andi's hand and shot a glare at Summer. "It's okay, Mom. I know what Dad's saying, though. Summer just waltzes in like she always does, while we've been here the whole time, contributing to the family business."

"Contributing?" Summer barked a humorless laugh. "Are you serious? You're not even paying the nominal rent you agreed to."

Jillian's face burned red. Gavin looked down guiltily.

Summer reined in her defensiveness and continued calmly. "You all need to understand what we're facing. It's the end of September. If we don't get this turned around, Willow Creek won't be here for New Year's."

"That's a lie!" Mack pounded a fist on the table.

Andi shook her head and quietly said, "No, it's not. Things really are that bad."

He scowled. "You're both exaggerating, and I won't have it. I'm not going to have anyone come in here and tell me my business."

"Dad, I'm not blaming anyone for anything. We are where we are, and we need to work forward from here. This is what I'm trained to do. You don't have to feel—"

He jabbed a finger in her direction. "Don't you tell me how to feel. You'll never have to worry about your kid looking you in the face and telling you you're a failure."

Everyone gasped, then a deafening silence settled over the kitchen. Even Jillian's mouth hung open as they all gaped at him.

It took a beat, but the color drained from Mack's face the

instant he realized what he'd said. "That's—That isn't—" he sputtered. "I didn't mean— That's not what—"

Summer's entire body went numb. It was such a low blow that she couldn't even process it. The chair scratched unnaturally loud against the floor as she pushed it back and stood. Every footstep on the old linoleum floor sounded like a heavy stomp in the stillness. No one even dared breathe.

"Summer—"

She ignored him and picked up her purse. She barely felt it in her hand.

"Summer, wait," Andi called after her.

Voices and chaotic noise collapsed in on the silence. Summer walked out the door and closed it softly behind her. She walked across the grass, her sneakers getting wetter with each step, and left footprints on the driveway as she crossed over to the crappy loaner Grand Am. It fired up with a bang.

She carefully pulled out of the driveway and reached over to crank the radio up. For an hour, she drove aimlessly around town, down some back roads that all connected somewhere, singing at the top of her lungs, because what else could she do?

Having a hysterectomy in her early twenties was just a fact of life. She'd come to terms with it a long time ago, and most of the time it didn't bother her at all. She supposed she hadn't hit that ticking biological clock the way most of the women she knew had, and there wasn't some deep longing for children. Sometimes she inevitably wondered how different her life would have been. Sometimes she had to answer invasive, nosey questions. But this? This was a punch straight to the gut.

The gas gauge dipped below quarter of a tank, so she figured she'd better find somewhere to park. The last place she wanted to go was home.

A few minutes later, she found herself pulling into a

familiar driveway. She parked the car and reached for the key to turn it off, then second-guessed herself. She hadn't known about Ben's business or anything that had been going on in his life, really. What if he had a girlfriend? Or a fiancé? Or a wife?

She had no business coming here. She put her hand on the gear shift just as the porch light flicked on. Ben came outside and called, "Summer?"

She wasn't sure what to do, so she sat there like a lump and did nothing.

Ben came off the porch and walked over to her car. "Come on in."

Chapter Eleven

Ben wasn't sure what to make of the situation. Why was she here? He didn't dare to hope she had suddenly appeared to profess her undying love, even though that would be awesome.

She shivered in her thin shirt.

"Where's your jacket?"

"I didn't think to grab it. I just had to get out of there." She hugged her arms around herself.

Ben led her into the kitchen and popped a coffee pod into the machine. While it came to life and sputtered hot coffee into the mug, he watched her from the corner of his eye.

She looked around the kitchen. "Looks a lot different than I remember. The cabinets are gorgeous."

He reached up and touched the hickory cabinet door above his coffeemaker. "Yeah, when my parents sold me the house I told them I was making changes so I didn't want to hear any complaints."

"Your mom didn't have anything to say when you gutted her kitchen?"

He laughed a little, remembering his mom's steadfast

determination to bite her tongue when he was knocking down walls and combining the kitchen and dining room. The only time she offered an unsolicited opinion was when he'd been looking at cabinets. He wasn't too proud to admit she'd been right, and he was glad he'd listened to her. "She did great. And after it was done she gave me her stamp of approval. She loves it so much she bakes her fifty billion Christmas cookies here." The machine sputtered the last drops of coffee into the mug. He handed it to her.

"Thanks." She lifted the mug slightly.

"She shows up with her church friends and they take over my kitchen and bake all day long. I get run out of town for the day, but I get paid in cookies, so I think I get the better end of the deal."

"She doesn't make them at her place?"

"Eh, her kitchen is pretty small. When they downsized, they *really* downsized." He waited a beat, then said, "You okay?"

"Yeah. No." She bobbed her head back and forth. "Maybe. I'm just frustrated. With everything. It feels like a million things have happened in such a short amount of time and I guess I'm having a hard time keeping everything under control."

He pushed out a breath that wasn't quite a laugh. "Control is an illusion."

"I suppose." She blew across the top of the coffee. "I'm sorry for barging in. It occurred to me when I was in your driveway that I wasn't even aware you had started your own company, so I really don't know if you have a girlfriend or fiancée or wife that wouldn't be too pleased with me being here."

"They're all out of town," he joked.

That got her to smile. "Funny."

"Nope, no wife, no fiancé, no girlfriend. Just me, myself, and I. Single and ready to mingle. Free as a bird."

"Think you could cram any more clichés into one breath?"

"I probably could." He waited a beat. "What happened?"

"Everything. I'm just exhausted and so, so tired of everyone being mad at me."

"Who's mad?"

She tilted her head and looked at him like it should be obvious.

"Your dad."

"Bingo." She stared into the coffee. "It kind of all blew up tonight. He's livid about the sign being fixed, even though it's not really about the sign at all. I'm trying so hard to consider his feelings and see where he's coming from, but I'm out of bandwidth. I can barely handle my own crap. I'm still getting nasty messages, I don't have my own vehicle, I had to wipe out most of my savings to move hundreds of miles at the drop of a hat, I got fired for the first time in my entire life, I'm trying to fix everything here, all my favorite stuff is in storage, and I can't even have dinner with my family without ticking somebody off."

He reached over and put a hand on her arm. "Summer. You've been back less than a week. I know you want to hit the ground running and fix everything, but listen to me. This stuff didn't happen overnight, and you're not going to course correct overnight. Your first priority needs to be taking care of yourself. Set reasonable hours. Spend time outside. Do something fun. You can't let the farm consume you, because that's how we get overwhelmed and end up like this, right?"

"Yeah." Her voice was barely a whisper.

"How do you eat an elephant?"

One corner of her mouth quirked up. "One bite at a time."

"Right. So what straw broke your camel's back tonight?"

"Oh, for Pete's sake. We've gone from clichés to animal comparisons?"

"I can do both if you'd like. You've been busy as a bee, but now you're on a wild goose chase in this dog eat dog world. We need to teach some old dogs some new tricks. Once we get your ducks in a row, it'll be like shooting fish in a barrel."

"Ben!" She laughed.

That was all he wanted. "I see you're getting mad as a hornet."

"Oh my gosh, Ben, stop."

"Well, now, hold your horses. I have more."

"No, please." She set the mug on the table and got serious again. "My dad made a comment about not having kids."

All humor vanished. "What?"

"He was mad that I'm coming in and making changes and he had a huge temper tantrum at dinner and ended up saying I'd never have to worry about my kid coming in and telling me how to run things."

Ben saw red. He loved Mack, he did, but right now he'd love nothing more than to knock him on his ass.

"I felt so blindsided."

"Of course you did. You don't expect people who love you to weaponize your medical history." He didn't know all the details about her health, just that she'd had to undergo a complete hysterectomy when she was in her early twenties. She seemed to have made her peace with not having kids, but before her surgery, she'd always been very open about wanting to have them.

"Wow. That's exactly what happened, isn't it?"

"Yes, it is, and it's completely unacceptable."

"I'm so torn, Ben. I'm so mad. So, so mad. And hurt. I know he didn't mean it the way it came out, but I just don't have the energy to not be upset."

"You should be upset." He put his hands over hers, which were still wrapped around the mug. "You know I love your dad like he's my own. But he's a grown-ass adult and can learn how to manage his temper and his mouth. I know he's frustrated and probably scared because he's got some big health issues and he isn't in control like he's been his whole life. That sucks, Summer, but he doesn't get to take it out on you."

She pulled on hand off the mug and put it over his. "Thanks, Ben."

"I'm here for you."

His phone vibrated in his pocket. He ignored it, but Summer stood up and said, "Bathroom in the same place?"

"Yeah."

After she walked away, he looked at his phone. Gavin. "Hello?"

"We can't find Summer. Have you heard from her?" The concern in Gavin's voice was palpable.

"She's here."

"Thank God. I was worried sick. Dad called a family meeting at dinner and kind of ambushed Summer with business stuff. Then he ended up making a nasty comment about she'd never know what it's like to have her kid call out her failures."

"He can't do that, Gav."

"I know, believe me. I lost my temper and I'm pretty sure this is the first time in my life I yelled at my father. Mom lost it. Nana's still crying, and even Jillian told him he was out of line." Gavin blew out a long breath. "Is she okay? She was so calm. That's what freaked me out the most. She just stood up and walked out. Didn't even slam the door. I've been calling her phone but she's not picking up."

"She's upset, but she's safe."

"I worry about her. She's so much like Mom, holding everything together and not letting anyone know when she's about to snap. Dad's a wreck. I've never seen him so upset."

"He should be."

"I know."

Ben heard Summer come back into the kitchen behind him. "I'll put you on speaker." He tapped his phone. "It's Gavin."

"Summer? You okay?"

"Yeah, I'm fine."

"Everybody's worried. What should I tell them?"

"You can tell them I'm fine."

"You need anything?"

"No, I'm good. Thanks."

Ben waited until they said their goodbyes and ended the call. "I'm sorry your dad said that."

Summer propped her elbows on the table and rested her chin in her hands. "I know he didn't mean it how it came out. As soon as he realized how it sounded, his face went pure white. But I just... it hurt regardless of what he was trying to say."

"Of course it did. You don't have to defend or justify him, Summer. He's a big boy and he needs to own his own crap. Not just this, but the business, too. He can keep his temper tantrums to himself." Mack was a great guy and had pretty much been his second dad, but he was only human and had some pretty big faults like everyone else.

"Thanks."

He reached over and rubbed her shoulder. "You're welcome to the guest room or the couch if you don't want to go back to the house tonight."

She leaned into his touch. "I appreciate it, but I think I'll head back home. And first thing tomorrow, I'm looking for an apartment. Too much togetherness isn't good for any of us."

"That's probably wise."

She stood up and held her arms out for a hug.

He nearly tripped over himself to get up and embrace her. He wished he could absorb all her hurt and worry.

"Thanks, Ben. I'm sorry to disrupt your evening with my drama."

He squeezed her tighter. "Don't apologize. My door's always open for you, Summer."

The words seemed to hang in the air until she pulled back and smiled. "Thanks again."

And then she was gone.

Chapter Twelve

The Grand Am announced her arrival with a giant bang as she turned the engine off. There'd be no sneaking around with this thing.

As soon as she went in the front door, her mom grabbed her in a tight hug. "Summer, where have you been?"

"Out."

Mack's face was blotchy and his eyes were red and watery. He hesitated behind Andi. "Summer, I'm sorry."

She took a step back, stunned. It was probably the first time in her life she'd heard her dad say those words. Usually when he knew he was wrong, he'd make up for it in his own way, but his way didn't include admitting his follies out loud.

"I never should have said something like that. I was trying to say—"

Summer held up a hand. She knew in her heart that he hadn't meant to be malicious, but she wasn't rewriting the past and acting like the words hadn't been said. "I get it, Dad. Stop explaining because it'll make it worse. I accept your apology, but right now I'm exhausted. Tomorrow we *are* having a come to Jesus meeting and things around here are going to change whether you like it or not. It's up to you whether I help fix things, or if I leave and the farm circles all the way down the drain."

He nodded his head slowly. "I'm sorry, Summer. I love you."

"Love you, too, Dad."

She turned to go up the stairs but stopped and turned back. "But you will never speak to me that way again."

Tuesday dawned bright and chilly. Summer pulled on her favorite hoodie and laced her sneakers. She was in the office before anyone else was awake, converting the ancient Excel 95 spreadsheets to the new format on her personal laptop.

She divided her lists into categories. Maintenance, safety, general business, and marketing were the main ones. Then she sorted everything into columns by urgency, color coded red, yellow, and green. In the end, the red and green columns each held a quarter of the list, with the remaining half creating a long column of yellow.

It was all busy work that didn't require a lot of thought. Which was perfect, because her stomach and her mind both churned over what was sure to be an unpleasant conversation.

Because she knew how it would look if she was in the comfy office chair facing them in folding chairs, she took a few minutes and set up one of the small square banquet tables that seat four people, so no one was sitting in a presumed position of power.

She printed three copies of her spreadsheet and put a cup of highlighters and pens on the table. She also printed three copies of the most up-to-date profit and loss statement. For emphasis, she color coded the negative numbers red. She nearly jumped out of her skin when the office door screeched open and her parents came in. Her dad was subdued. Her mother looked tired.

Without preamble, Summer took charge of the meeting. "I have no intention of rehashing the events of last evening. Dad, you said what you said, you apologized, and I accept. I think any further discussion will just make things worse. Besides, it was basically a symptom of a bigger issue we have."

They both looked at her expectantly.

"It's pretty clear to me that there was no general consensus of what was going to happen when I got home. I've already had this discussion with Mom, but it seems that we need to all get on the same page with no misunderstanding."

Andi nodded in agreement.

Mack shifted in his seat, but said nothing.

"Here's the deal." She slid copies of the profit and loss statements to each of her parents. "Here's the section of accounts with their current balances. These figures do include any outstanding checks that haven't come back yet, as well as automated payments through the end of the month that will come out. For right now, we're in good shape. The problem is here." She pointed to the next section. "This is where we would have expected income. As you can see, there's nothing coming in." She pulled in a deep breath and prepared to deliver the most awkward part of the conversation. "Including the agreed-upon rent from Batter Up! and Jilly's Blooms."

Both her parents shifted uncomfortably.

"This is just a snapshot of where we are, right this minute. It's a lot of red, but this can be fixed. We'll have to tighten our belts and choose our expenses wisely, but we can get through until spring on what we currently have. Now to the nitty gritty. I know how to get us out of this hole, and I am perfectly willing to stay and do my job and get it done. What I am not willing to do is listen to a bunch of grumbling and backstabbing and complaining about my methods or my authority. We're either all on board, or I'm going to start looking for another job today, and you're on your own to keep doing whatever you're doing."

Andi and Mack exchanged a look that she couldn't quite decipher.

She continued, "We have the same goal. To get Willow Creek back to holding weddings and bringing in money and being a top quality venue with outstanding attention to detail."

Mack sighed. "Most of this is my fault. I let too many balls drop."

Summer said, "There's no use in assigning any blame anywhere." She tapped the profit and loss. "This is just math. There's no judgment in math. We're here right now, and we need to change that."

"It's overwhelming," Andi said quietly.

"It doesn't have to be. If you can both let me do my job and manage the facility, there's a very clear path forward. I'm coming in this with a fresh set of eyes *and* a personal vested interest in Willow Creek's success. And business management is what I studied. I legitimately know what I'm doing."

Andi nudged Mack. "Might as well get our money's worth from her tuition, right?"

He managed a small smile. "Yeah. There's just so much that needs done. It's too much for one person to handle."

"Dad." Summer leaned forward and met his gaze. "Do you agree that I have the best interests of Willow Creek at heart?"

"Yes."

"Do you trust that I will not make major decisions without input from you and Mom?"

"Yes."

"Do you believe we share a similar vision of what Willow

Creek should be? Even if we have different methods, you do know that I wouldn't plan to use the farm for a traveling circus, right?"

"A traveling circus could be fun," Andi said.

Mack nodded. "Yes, I think we have a similar vision."

"Can you step back and let me do my job?"

He hesitated for a long moment. "Yeah, I can do that."

Summer held out a pinky. "Promise?"

He wrapped his pinky around hers. "Promise."

"Great. We have a lot of work to do." She handed each of them a clipboard and a pen. "These are the issues I've found. I have them color coded by urgency. Simple red, yellow, green system. I figured we could go over them, quickly, and there are spaces at the bottom to add anything I've missed. First up, the empty fire extinguisher in Willow Hall. Who do we contact for that?"

Mack cleared his throat. "I'll call them."

Summer opened her mouth, but he interrupted her.

"I'll call them *today*. We did have them inspected last year like we're supposed to, so I'll get some answers about why that one failed."

"Okay, great." She wrote "Dad" beside the item.

As they divvied up the red responsibilities, Summer began to relax. Her dad was being cooperative and even offered some suggestions. When she gently suggested creating a master contact list for the companies they used, he didn't object.

After an hour or so, she looked up from her sheet. "It looks like we can get these critical issues handled in the next few days, so let's stop there and meet again, say, Monday morning? We'll do a status report and then tackle the next section, okay?"

"Sounds good," Andi said.

"Yup." Mack tapped his page. "Did you happen to look at

fire extinguishers in the other buildings? If that one didn't hold its charge, others might be bad, too."

"No, I didn't."

He nodded. "I'll do that first, then make the call."

"Great."

He followed Andi out but paused in the doorway. He turned back and held up the clipboard. "For what it's worth, I think this is the right way to go about this. I've been trying to figure out a way to take care of everything at once and nothing ends up getting done that way. I'll try not to be so difficult."

"Thanks, Dad."

After he closed the door, Summer stared after him. Maybe there was hope for some progress on that front after all. He must have done some serious introspection after last night's outburst.

She was cleaning up some of her notes when her walkie talkie crackled.

"Summer?"

"Go ahead, Dad."

"The fire extinguisher company will be here next Tuesday and I'm heading out now to see Earl."

"Who's Earl?"

"My lightbulb guy."

He really did have a lightbulb guy. "Oh. I found a commercial bulb distributer online I was going to order from."

Mack grunted a little, like he wanted to argue but was biting his tongue.

Summer relented. She'd give him this one because it wasn't worth the conflict. "It's fine, I didn't place the order, so if you want to get from Earl, that works."

The walkie crackled again. "You wanna go along?"

Summer had no real desire to visit a lightbulb warehouse,

but she knew her dad was trying to make amends for his thoughtless comment and attitude in general.

He sweetened the deal. "We can stop by Dunkin' if you want."

Her forced smile turned genuine. "Absolutely."

Two hours later, she found herself humbled a little. Earl was not just some guy selling lightbulbs out of his garage. He owned an entire lighting company with a state of the art showroom, serving mostly commercial operations and new home construction, with a few clients like Willow Creek, who they supplied smaller services to.

Back in her dad's truck, Summer sipped her iced coffee. "Okay, you win that one."

Mack smirked and tapped his thumb on the steering wheel. "Is that so?"

"Yeah. As much as it pains me to admit, Earl's prices were competitive, and I'm so impressed that he checked every single bulb before letting us out the door. We definitely would have some broken bulbs from the online supplier."

"Well, how about that."

"You don't have to be so smug."

"I'm just savoring the moment." He grinned, then said, "I think we've both got a stubborn streak that's maybe causing some roadblocks. I'm really sorry for how I've been acting. It's hard to admit that maybe I haven't been doing things the right way for a long time. Just gets overwhelming at a certain point, you know?"

"I know." She reached over and squeezed his shoulder. "And I promise to be more open-minded about our suppliers."

"I'm sure there are a lot of things we can get cheaper and faster online, but it's really important to me that we support local businesses."

He was right. If their small business was to succeed, they

had to support other small, local businesses. Wasn't that a big part of the vision for Willow Creek? Yes, it was. "From now on we'll look local first."

"Deal."

They pulled back in the driveway with more than light-bulbs and fresh caffeine. She'd come back home with a weight lifted off her shoulders and a pretty huge barrier between them gone.

Way to go, Earl.

Chapter Thirteen

"Did you like it?" Ben asked his mom as they sat at her kitchen table.

Susie nodded. "Loved it. The way Gavin added that lemon zest right to the frosting was brilliant. Even better than his original recipe."

"Wow. I didn't think he'd ever top that one."

She chuckled. "I didn't, either."

"Doesn't seem fair. He's my friend but I don't get to taste test his cakes."

"Changing the subject a little, Gavin mentioned that Summer's back home. Have you seen her?"

"I'm guessing you know I have."

"Gavin also mentioned you've been over at the farm a bit more frequently the past week or so. I'm sure there's no connection, though." She eyed him over the rim of her coffee cup.

She was as subtle as a freight train. "Slight connection. I had to quit mowing when she got here last week because she needed help moving her stuff. I had to go back and finish the mowing. Then I fixed the sign and had to go back over to hang it."

"Well, *I'm* convinced," she said with a laugh.

"If you're done, ma'am, I'll take a look at that cracked board on your deck."

She snickered and walked to the back door.

Ben followed her outside. "When did you get new cushions?" He patted the porch swing.

"Last weekend."

"Nice. I like the color." The blue striped pattern went really well with the outdoor rug his parents had gotten several months earlier.

Susie walked over and wiggled the handrail. "Right here. It cracked all the way through."

Ben inspected the board. "I see that."

"What would have caused that? It was fine before."

"Could be anything, but I'm betting this board was just a dud and when it dried and shrunk, it cracked more than it should have."

"Can you fix it?"

"Of course. I'll run over to the shop and see what I have on hand." He rubbed his chin. "It's a pretty big job. It's gonna cost you."

She crossed her arms. "How much?"

He reached out and touched the board and made a concerned face. "Oooh, this looks like a pork chop and baked potato job."

She jabbed a finger at his nose. "Extortion. That's what this is. Taking advantage of a defenseless little old lady. I should turn you in."

He laughed and grabbed her finger, tugging her against his side for a hug. "Defenseless! You're about as defenseless as a cobra with a chainsaw."

"Don't be ridiculous. A cobra doesn't have arms to use a chainsaw." She chuckled and patted his back. "Seriously, though, you can't go around doing jobs for free. That's not wise business."

He'd heard this argument a million times. "Moommm. I don't do jobs for free."

"Well, pork chops is hardly fair compensation."

"*And* a baked potato. And green beans with the bacon and that sauce you used to make. And some warm chocolate chip cookies. With ice cream."

She laughed. "Okay, okay, I'm sorry I said anything." She flicked her wrist up to look at her watch. "Too late in the day for all that, so I'll pay you tomorrow night."

Ben held the door open as they walked back inside.

"*After* the job is done to my satisfaction," she added.

"You drive a hard bargain for such a little old lady. Maybe I should speak to the man of the house."

She swatted his arm. "Get out of here."

Ben gave his head a shake as he jumped into his truck. He was very grateful for his relationship with his parents. Some of his friends had horror story relationships with their families, and/or with their in-laws. It certainly wasn't that they never got on each other's nerves, because they definitely did from time to time, but he'd always known that his parents loved both him and his sister, Jenna.

When he got to his shop, he parked and went inside.

"Hey, Boss," his office manager, Diane said. She turned her attention back to the man standing near her desk. "You're in luck. This is the guy you'd need to speak with. Ben, this is Isaiah."

"Isaac," the man corrected.

"Sorry." She grimaced.

Isaac didn't seem affronted. "Happens all the time." He held out his hand to Ben. "Isaac Frazier."

Ben shook his hand. "Ben Keller. I only have a minute. What can I do for you?"

Isaac pulled a business card and a flyer out of his black leather messenger bag. "I'm a small business consultant from the Frazier Foundation. I'm in the area visiting some different small businesses. I was just at Gino's Body Shop and he suggested I come see you."

Okay, if Gino sent the guy his way, he must not be a regular salesman. "We can step into my office for a minute."

"Great."

Inside Ben's tiny office, Isaac took the folding chair in front of the desk. Ben dropped into his rickety, hardly used office chair. "What is it you do?"

Isaac gave a brief overview. "The main thing we do is give small grants for things like equipment, software, or inventory. We also offer low interest loans, mostly for brand new businesses that the bank won't touch. We also offer consultations, where we sit with owners and/or managers and go over ways to increase profitability and efficiency."

Ben looked down at the flyer. "Grants? Isn't that a government thing? Are you actually just a middle man or something?"

"No. We definitely do have information on government grants if you're interested, because they're out there but hard to find if you don't know precisely what you're looking for. These grants are through us, and have much less red tape."

"I guess I don't get why you'd just hand out free money."

Isaac grinned. "I get that lot. The Frazier Foundation is the philanthropic arm of Frazier Industries, which if you're not familiar, was started as a small business by my great-great grandmother in 1930, right at the start of the Great Depression. Long story short, from the first dollar she made, she carved out half to serve others. In the 1970s, the company had grown so much that my grandmother and her brother made the phil-anthropic arm a completely separate entity. It's still overseen by the same board of directors and whatnot, but being sepa-rate allows for greater focus on both sides."

Ben nodded. He'd definitely heard of Frazier Industries. "If it's all about philanthropy, why aren't you giving money to charities?"

"We do, of course, but our main mission is to help small businesses, which are a huge benefit to their communities, which in turn helps local charities in the long run. I have statistics if you'd like to see them."

"Why here?"

Isaac answered with a smile. "Kind of a dart on the map, to be honest. We focus more on rural areas that might be under-served by other organizations that support small businesses, and Willow Creek fit our criteria. So here I am, visiting a variety of establishments and introducing myself."

Ben studied the flyer for a long moment. "I really could have used you four years ago. Now, though, it doesn't look like there's a lot we can..." He trailed off. "These equipment grants. What kind of hoops do you have to jump through?"

Isaac shrugged one shoulder. "We have an application to fill out, and then the grant covers specific items. You have to provide proof of how the money was used within thirty days, otherwise it converts to a low-interest loan. It's a fairly straightforward process."

"Would it cover something like a new computer?"

"Absolutely. Anything that's legitimate business equipment."

He sat back in his chair. "You work with all kinds of small businesses? Like a farm-turned-event-venue?"

Isaac looked a little confused. "Sure."

"I don't need your services right now, but I know someone who might."

Chapter Fourteen

Summer couldn't figure out why Isaac Frazier, bazillionaire and world's most eligible bachelor, was standing in the lobby of The Shoppes.

"Hi. Can I help you?" She set her armload of linens on the counter and reached out to shake his hand.

"Hi. Isaac Frazier."

She nodded with a grin. "Yeah. I know who you are."

Isaac bowed his head a little. "I'm afraid you find me at a bit of a disadvantage then."

"Sorry. Summer Sullivan."

"And you're the owner of all this?" He waved a hand to encompass everything.

"No, I'm the facility manager. My parents own the business."

"Willow Creek Weddings, correct?"

"Yes."

He looked around thoughtfully. "Do you host other events? Birthdays, bar or bat mitzvahs, baby showers, vendor events?"

"Um, not really? We focus mostly on weddings." She felt like he'd smacked her in the brain with a two by four. Why put all their eggs in the wedding basket? Why hadn't she thought of that herself?

"Your parents also own these?" He pointed to the doors leading to Jilly's Blooms and Batter Up!. "They really have the trifecta here for weddings. Venue, flowers, cake. Nice."

"Actually, my sister owns the flower shop and my brother owns the bakery. They're separate entities."

"Interesting."

Summer crossed her arms, but thought that might seem too aggressive so she tucked her hands into her pockets. "What brings you here?"

Isaac's attention suddenly snapped back to her. "We've met. At my cousin Francesca's wedding."

"Yes. I was her wedding planner."

He smiled. "I knew you looked familiar. You plan weddings in Chicago? From here?"

She straightened her back. "No. I recently left Chicago and moved back here."

He nodded. "I can see why. This area is stunning. The changing leaves are really something."

She couldn't get over the fact that Isaac Frazier was standing in her lobby. "I'm sorry," she said, "what can I help you with?"

"Sorry. I'm a little distracted. There's a lot to look at." He gestured to Jillian's display case.

"My sister does incredible bouquets." It was true. Jillian might not be her favorite person, but Summer could easily admit her sister was incredibly talented with flowers.

"I'm hoping that I can help you, actually." He handed her a flyer and a business card. "The owner of Keller Construction said you might be interested in taking a look at what we have to offer."

It took a few seconds for Summer to connect Keller

Construction with Ben. "He did?" How on earth did Ben know Isaac Frazier? "I have to admit, I'm a little confused. How do you know Ben?"

"I don't."

The confusion on her face must have been clear.

"Let me start from the beginning. Can we sit?"

"Of course, sorry." She gestured to the high stools at the counter.

They sat and Isaac gave his spiel about the Frazier Foundation and its mission.

"And that is how I ended up here."

Her lists flitted through her mind. If they could get a grant for some new equipment, that would not only make things in her office run more smoothly, it would take some pressure off their budget for upcoming expenses. "I have to admit, it all sounds good, but it sounds too good to be true. And you know what they say about that."

"I do. Which is why I have an extensive list of references or testimonials or whatever you'd like to call them. I'd encourage you to contact any of them." He rifled in his messenger bag.

Jillian came in the main doors carrying a tray of sunflowers. She shot a "who's that" look to Summer.

"Isaac, this is my sister, Jillian, the owner of Jilly's Blooms."

Isaac looked up. The page of references slipped from his hand and fluttered to the floor. He jumped off his seat and scrambled to pick them up. "Hi."

"Hello. Nice to meet you," Jillian said, once he was done fumbling around.

He nodded.

"I'd shake your hand but..." She inclined her head toward the tray.

"Hi."

"Hi?"

"I'm Frazier. Isaac. Isaac Frazier."

"Jillian Sullivan."

Summer watched Isaac's face with a little amusement. He was clearly smitten with her sister. "He's a small business consultant with the Frazier Foundation. They do grants and loans and stuff."

"Loans? We don't need to be getting into debt," Jillian warned.

Oh, look, they agreed on something. That was a pleasant surprise.

He fumbled in his messenger bag without ever taking his eyes off Jillian. "We, um, it's not just loans. In fact, that's just a small part of what we do. We do a lot of consulting. Meetings. With business owners. To, um, business plans and... business owners." He pulled out another flyer and held it out to Jillian.

She raised an eyebrow and inclined her head toward the tray of sunflowers again.

"Oh. Yes. Sorry. Can I carry these for you?" He set the flyer on the counter.

"Thanks, but I got it." She shot Summer a "what is with this guy" look and went into her shop.

Isaac turned his attention back to Summer. He must have realized he'd been caught staring at Jillian, because his cheeks and tips of his ears reddened. "Sorry. Where was I?"

Summer wanted to make a sarcastic joke about him ogling her sister, but she suppressed the urge. "References. You were about to give me a list of your references."

"Ah! Yes. Sorry, I got distracted." He lifted the flap on his bag and pulled out a folder.

She bit her lips together to keep from laughing. Distracted was an understatement.

"Here they are." He slipped a sheet of paper out of the folder and handed it to her.

She glanced down to an impressive list of businesses with the owners' names and phone numbers. "Thanks. I'll make some phone calls. How long are you in the area?"

"At least a week. Maybe a little longer. Willow Creek has an impressive number of small businesses." He huffed a little laugh. "Which you well know since there are three of them right here, right?"

"Right."

"I'll leave another packet for your other sister? The bakery?"

"Brother. And I can just show him this." She held up the papers he'd already given her.

"Okay, great. I'll check back in with you in a couple days, or you can call me any time."

"Sounds good." She walked him to the doors and watched as he got in his car and pulled out of the parking lot.

"What was with that guy?" Jillian asked, coming up behind Summer to peer out the glass doors and watch Isaac leave.

"I think you got him flustered."

Jillian rolled her eyes. "Yeah, right."

"Ben sent him over. I'm going to call some of these references. If we can get a grant to cover a few things, that'd be amazing."

"Just watch the fine print."

"Absolutely." Summer tried not to assume her sister was being patronizing, but given their history, it was difficult.

"Don't be getting us deeper in debt."

She pulled in a deep breath and held it for a count of five. Not one penny of the farm's existing debt had been Summer's doing. She decided not to repeat the suggestion that the flower shop and bakery to start paying the rent they were supposed to be contributing and settled on, "Yep."

Before Summer could be subjected to any more sage advice, she went upstairs to the office and closed the door.

The first call she made was to Ben. "Thanks for sending him my way. I'm looking through the stuff he left me, and they have a specific grant for office equipment."

"If you could get a new computer, that'd be great. By the way, I talked to Jeff, and he was able to pull some of your files off the laptop. He saved them on a new hard drive and he's going to drop it by my place tomorrow evening."

"That's awesome, please let me know what I owe. Maybe this means things are looking up, because Gino just texted me to let me know my car's done."

"Maybe he'll let you keep the Grand Am and you can let him keep your Escape."

She laughed. "I'd feel guilty taking advantage of him like that."

"Good point. Maybe if you give him the Escape and a few hundred bucks?"

"Anything I'd offer would be a lowball. This Grand Am has almost three hundred thousand miles on it and it's still running. It's probably immortal."

"The funny part is that I bet the odometer's been rolled back at least once, too."

"No doubt." She paused, then changed the subject. "Are you busy?"

"I'm at mom and dad's fixing the back porch railing, why?"

"Isaac said something that got me thinking, so I was wondering if I could run some things by you."

"Shoot."

"I meant in person. I don't want anyone to overhear."

Chapter Fifteen

"Yeah, no problem. Do you want to meet me at Rosie's at five?"

"Great. I'll see you there."

Ben stared down at his phone before he slipped it into his pocket. What ideas could Isaac Frazier have put in her head that she didn't want to be overheard?

He leveled the board against the railing. Perfect.

The door slid open behind him. "How's it going?"

"Hey, Dad," Ben said over his shoulder. "Good."

"Need a hand?"

He didn't, but he said, "Sure. Will you hold this?"

Charlie held the drill while Ben tapped the board into place with a hammer. "You staying for dinner?"

"I can't. I'm meeting Summer at Rosie's."

"Finally got the nerve to ask her out, did you? It's about time."

Ben looked up in surprise just as he swung the hammer down. He whacked his thumb. "Ouch!" Luckily he'd only been tapping and not beating something into place. He dropped the hammer onto the top step and squeezed his thumb.

"You okay?"

"Yeah." He shook his hand out. "Why would you think I asked her out?"

Charlie gave an amused snort-laugh. "Because you've been pining for her for years and now she's finally back home. Kind of a no-brainer."

Ben focused on screwing the board into place. "I haven't."

"You should."

"It's not like the thought hasn't crossed my mind."

"What are you waiting for?"

"She just got out of a relationship. She's busy with the farm."

"Blah, blah, blah."

"And she still only thinks of me as an extra little brother."

"So change her mind."

Ben popped the lid open on the can of paint. "Hand me that brush."

Charlie set the drill down and gave Ben the brush.

He swiped paint on the new board. "I'll do a second coat tomorrow after this one dries."

"Nonsense. I can handle painting. Nice subject change, by the way."

Ben shrugged his shoulders. "No idea what you're talking about. Oh look at the time, I have to run, but it's been great."

Charlie took the paint can from him. "Good luck."

"Dad. We're just talking business."

Laughing, Charlie said, "Yeah, yeah. Go on then, you don't want to be late for your *meeting*."

Well before five, he slid into a booth at Rosie's Diner, one where he had a good view of the front door. He was halfway through his soda and scrolling through his phone when John Forester plopped down across from him.

"Yo, Benny, what's up?"

"I'm waiting for someone."

"Oh yeah? A lady?" He wiggled his eyebrows and leered. "Who?"

Ben sighed. "Summer."

"Summer. Summer... You mean Summer Sullivan?"

"Yeah."

John perked up. "Dang, I didn't know she was back in town. You hitting that? Niiiiice." He held his fist across the table for a bump.

Ben halfheartedly grazed his knuckles against John's. "No, I'm not hitting that."

John's face split into a huge grin. "Sweet. Maybe Johnny'll give it a shot." He reached out and tapped the arm of the waitress passing by. "Hey, Sweetheart, bring me a water." Without pausing for a breath, he said, "You been fishing? The bites out Hopper Creek are craayyyzeee."

"No, I haven't had time."

"Aw, you gotta make time for stuff like that."

The waitress set a glass of water on the table. "Here you go, Johnny."

"Thanks, babe."

She didn't bother to disguise her eyeroll. "Refill, Ben?"

"Sure, thanks."

She took his glass and brought it back a moment later.

"Is Summer seeing anybody?"

Ben shrugged. "I have no idea."

"Whoa, that her?" He pointed out the window.

Ben looked and saw Summer at the far side of the parking lot getting out of her Escape. He nodded. "Yeah."

"Take a look at those hips. Mmm mmm. Watch and learn, boy. Johnny's gonna show you how it's done." He launched into a story about his latest fishing expedition, which included lots of hand gestures to demonstrate how big the fish were.

Ben saw it coming and part of him wanted to give a warning. A very, very small part. That was overruled.

John's hand whacked his water, sending a gush straight down into his own lap. "Dang it!" He leaped to his feet.

Ben grabbed the glass before it could roll onto the floor.

"I'll be right back." He hustled toward the restroom just as Summer came in the door.

Ben saw him say something to her, but his view was blocked by the waitress bringing a cloth to wipe up the water.

"That guy," she muttered.

Ben scrambled out of the booth and grabbed his drink. He gestured to the one directly behind him. "I'm going to move to this table if you don't mind."

"No problem. This'll take a minute to dry anyway."

Summer came around the waitress and over to Ben. "What happened? Johnny wanted to give me a hug, but he was all wet." She made a face.

Not that Ben thought Summer would ever actually go on a date with John, but stranger things had happened. He blurted out, "He peed himself again."

"What?" She slid into the dry booth and leaned toward him. "No way."

"Yeah, it happens every now and then when he gets all excited. He's pretty sensitive about it so I wouldn't say anything."

She matched his whisper. "What was he worked up about?"

"He was telling me about his latest fishing trip up Hopper Creek."

"Wow."

John appeared beside their table and leaned toward Summer. "Hey, gorgeous, I haven't seen you in a hot minute. You look *smokin'*. Where you been?"

"Chicago."

"Nice. How long you home for?"

Summer shrugged and leaned away from him. "Not sure yet."

"Sweet Summmmmer. Gimme your digits." He pulled his phone out and grimaced. "Aw man, I gotta bounce. Mom's been texting me and she gets all irrational if I'm not home by dinner." He winked and pointed a finger at Summer. "We'll connect real soon, babe."

Summer raised her eyebrows. "Bye, John."

Ben managed to keep a straight face. "I mean, he *is* kind of an upgrade from that chef guy."

She burst out a surprised laugh. "I'm not sure I'd go that far."

They ordered their food and after Summer got her soda, Ben asked, "What's up?"

"Isaac Frazier. When he was at the farm, he asked me if we did events other than weddings."

"Yeah?" He didn't understand why this was significant.

"It seems like such a no-brainer and I'm a little baffled as to why we didn't ever think of expanding."

Ben tapped his fingertips on the table. "Maybe they did think of it? Maybe there's a complication with insurance or something?"

"Maybe," she said thoughtfully. "I'll have to suggest it to Mom and see what she says. If we expanded to doing bridal showers and baby showers, that would certainly bring in some income. I mean, we've done some, but it's not something we ever advertised as an option. He also mentioned vendor events, and that really got the wheels turning. That's significant income from the vendors just for their booth space, and we'd just have the cost of staff."

"Do you think your parents want to shift the focus away from weddings?"

She pointed to herself. "I don't want to shift the focus so much as expand it. And more events means more exposure, which should translate ultimately to more weddings."

He could easily see where she was coming from. He wasn't so sure her parents would be on board, even if it was a good idea. And it did sound like a good idea, but this was outside his wheelhouse, so there were probably downsides he'd never think of.

"I guess I wanted confirmation that it's not a crazy idea before I go stirring the pot."

"Makes sense to me. Maybe bring it up like... hey, did we ever think of doing these events? and see how they respond. Have you looked at other venues to see what they're doing?"

"See? That's why called you. I was so focused on how we might do things I hadn't even looked at what anyone else is doing. I'll do that before I talk to Mom." She leaned over her plate and lowered her voice. "In other news, I think Isaac Frazier has a thing for my sister."

He leaned in. "Why?"

"We were in the lobby talking and when Jillian came in he got all flustered and could barely get his name out. It was adorable. Gave me Bingley and Jane vibes."

"Who?"

Summer rolled her eyes. "*Pride and Prejudice.*"

Ben frowned. He must be remembering it wrong. "I thought that was Darcy."

"It is. Bingley is Darcy's best friend. And Jane is Elizabeth's older sister."

He vaguely remembered the movie. "Ah. Is he the guy with the potatoes?"

"You can't be serious. That's Mr. Collins, who is the cousin that's trying to marry Elizabeth. He ends up marrying Elizabeth's best friend, Charlotte Lucas."

He held up a hand. "Don't get mad. I haven't seen the movie since it first came out."

"The one with Keira Knightley?"

"Of course."

Summer rolled her eyes again. "Of *course*. That came out in 2005. How have you not watched it since?"

Ben cocked his head. "Okay, Miss Judgypants, how many times have you seen *Rocky*? *The Godfather*? They're classic, exactly like your *Pride and Prejudice*."

"Exactly? Okay, who was the brilliant and acclaimed author who wrote the book *Rocky* was based on?"

"Wasn't based on a book. It was loosely based on a real-life boxer. Chuck Wepner, who almost beat Muhammad Ali. Written by the brilliant and acclaimed Sylvester Stallone. And I'm sure you know *The Godfather* was based on the book by Mario Puzo. Who, by the way, was also brilliant and acclaimed."

"Okay, you get a point for that, but he's not on the same level as Jane Austen."

"Only because she had a hundred-year head start."

"I don't even know how to respond to that."

"I'll take that as a win."

"You shouldn't."

Ben poked at his fries and realized opportunity had just knocked at his door. Now was as good a time as any. "How about this? Movie day on Saturday. We watch either *Rocky* or *The Godfather,* and then we watch *Pride and Prejudice*. Expand both our horizons."

Summer narrowed her eyes. "I get to pick the version."

He didn't know what to make of the wicked grin she was wearing, but that sounded like a yes, so he didn't care.

Chapter Sixteen

By the time Saturday rolled around, Summer was beyond ready to get away from the farm for a bit. She pulled into the driveway of Ben's two-story house a little before eleven. She grabbed her tote bag off the passenger seat and went up the stairs to the big front porch. Susie's prize ferns hung above the railing, thick and lush and green.

Before she could knock, Ben pulled the door open.

Summer gestured to the ferns. "I see you've inherited your mom's green thumb."

He came out on the porch with her. "Not even a little bit. Mom comes over and takes care of them. The other day she said something about 'overwintering' them soon." He made air quotes around the word. "All I know is that I have to carry them to their special designated spot in the basement the minute she sees frost in the forecast. I've offered to put up hooks at her new house, but she said something about her porch getting the wrong kind of sun, whatever that means."

"Beats me. Plants come to me to die. I tried a spider plant in my apartment because they're supposedly easy to care for. Not easy enough, apparently, because the thing turned brown in like a week. My friend who gave it to me was horrified. She took it back and made me promise to never get another plant that wasn't plastic or fabric, although I could probably find a way to kill them, too. Easy promise to make. Never again."

"Mom told me when she passes I might as well bury these with her because there's no way I'll take good care of them."

"Ouch. Morbid, but probably accurate."

He held the screen door open for her.

Summer paused right inside the door to toe her shoes off onto the rug that held Ben's sneakers and work boots. "This weather is so crazy. It was so bright and sunny two hours ago, and now it looks like it wants to storm."

"I think it's calling for rain."

She walked over to the couch and reached into her tote bag. "I wasn't sure if you still had a DVD player or not, so I brought one."

"No, Summer, I don't have a DVD player." He joked, "I stream everything because it's the twenty-first century. In fact, I have *Rocky* all queued up and ready to go. No disc required."

"Ooh hoo hoo, I didn't realize you were the king of technology."

"And I didn't realize you were a luddite."

"Nice. Was that on your word a day calendar?" she teased.

"Ha, ha. I'm not the one running around with a DVD player. What if you got carjacked? If they knew the right black market antiques dealer, they'd be set for life."

She opened her mouth to spar back, but he snapped his fingers and ran for the kitchen just as a timer went off. She followed him and watched as he took something out of the oven. "What's that?"

"Nachos. I even put jalapeños on half, just for you." He held out the tray of nachos for her to see.

"That looks amazing." It really did. Tortilla chips lined the baking sheet, covered with taco-seasoned ground beef, chunks of chicken, and lots of melted cheese, with circles of jalapeños dotting half of the tray.

"Salsa, sour cream, and guac in the fridge if you want to grab them."

"You got it." She got the items and set them on the counter beside the stove.

"I also have garlic parmesan wings in the fridge to make between movies," he said as he sprinkled chopped tomatoes and green peppers over the nachos.

"I didn't know we were being this fancy. I would have made something instead of just bringing a packet of microwave popcorn."

"Well there you go, because I don't have any popcorn."

She inhaled deeply. "I have to admit, the nachos are way better than microwave popcorn."

"I even found these at the dollar store." He handed her a plastic plate that was divided into a large section and two smaller sections. "To keep your salsa separate from your guac."

Summer looked down at the plate and shook her head. "How on earth did you remember that?"

"Core memory. When someone screams and throws an entire bowl of salsa at you, you tend to remember that person's preferences. Especially when the salsa lands all over your favorite Celtics jersey."

Summer put her hands over her face. She remembered that day. "Ben. I'm sorry. I was thirteen. I thought you had forgiven me."

"Oh, I have. Decades ago. Doesn't mean I've forgotten such a traumatic experience. And I bet you still don't like your salsa to touch your guac, do you?"

"I can't argue with that. But I promise I wouldn't have thrown the bowl at you."

He snickered. "You've learned some decorum as you've aged?"

"Don't push it."

"Come on, Rocky's waiting for us."

They loaded up their plates and went into the living room. Summer sat on the couch and curled her legs under her. "These nachos are amazing."

On the other end of the couch, Ben nodded. "Thanks. I rolled the tortillas myself to make the chips."

She eyed him suspiciously. "Really? So the empty Tostitos bag was what, inspiration?"

He laughed around a hefty bite of nachos. "Yup. I even threshed the wheat."

"From the crop you grew in your back yard?"

"Obviously."

"Okay, Farmer Ben. Start the movie."

She half-watched the movie as she ate and let her mind wander. This was nice. Better than nice. For the first time in almost a month, she felt completely relaxed. Being busy and all the family drama had kept her mind off the Chicago situation. She'd texted with Kayla a few times, but with the farm and Kayla inheriting Summer's brides, they were both extremely busy.

She'd also made the mistake of checking her social media inboxes. The nasty messages from strangers had almost, but not quite, died out.

Summer shook her head and focused on the movie instead of things she couldn't do anything about from Chicago. She winced every time Rocky took a punch. "Why would anyone want to go into boxing? It's so brutal."

"Same as any other sport."

"I'm not denying the athleticism. But in soccer the point is to kick the ball into the goal. In boxing, the goal is to beat the crap out of your opponent."

"Actually, a lot of the goal is to keep yourself from being hit. There's a lot of strategy involved. It really is a legitimate sport."

"I totally agree that it is. I'm just saying I don't get it, which isn't a criticism. I mean, I also don't get why people want to go running or swallow swords or be a train conductor. No shade, it's just not my thing. Probably because I like my face the way it is. Don't want my nose rearranged."

"I'll give you that one. I actually like watching boxing and UFC and all that, but I wouldn't participate." He lifted his chin and patted his cheeks. "Can't mess up the money maker."

Summer laughed. "Nope, you're way too pretty for boxing."

"Shh, the best part's coming up."

She side-eyed him for shushing her, but turned her attention back to the movie. A few minutes later, she held her hands over her eyes, peeking through her fingers, not wanting to watch, but not able to look away as Rocky and Apollo Creed pummeled each other until their faces were swollen and battered.

And then the fight was over. The crowd rushed into the boxing ring, with announcers and security. Rocky ignored them all and called for Adrian.

Summer was riveted, listening as the winner was announced. Apollo Creed. Adrian climbed into the ring and she and Rocky professed their love for one another. The credits rolled.

"Hold up. He didn't win."

Ben smiled like he knew something she didn't. "He *did* win. No, he didn't win the match, but he made it all fifteen rounds. That was his goal, and he attained it."

Summer nodded slowly, understanding the point. "He didn't need to beat Apollo Creed to win. I got it. That's actually pretty clever. Most movies have the hero getting everything they wanted."

"He did get everything he wanted. His goal was to prove he could go toe to toe for fifteen rounds. That was what he wanted. Winning or losing was irrelevant. I mean, Rocky had no business getting as far as he did. But he did it. And, of course, he got the girl."

Chapter Seventeen

Ben said, "Did you enjoy it? Overall?"

"Oh, for sure. I saw it a long, long time ago, but I didn't really remember it. And there's a lot more nuance than I expected. I'd give it a six point five out of ten."

"That's pretty good. I'm glad you liked it." He glanced at his watch. Five after one. "Are you hungry? It's up to you if you want me to make the wings now or after your movie."

"We could have the wings now and order pizza later. The movie won't be over until about six."

"Six? It's only one o'clock." Was she planning on watching it three times?

Summer slid the DVD case out of her tote bag. "You said I could pick the version. I picked this one."

Colin Firth judged him from the cover of the case.

"Oh, boy."

"It's five hours long. Really encompasses the novel in a very faithful way."

He made some grumbling noises, but the fact remained that Summer was going to be here, hanging out, for the next five hours. On purpose. That was a good sign, right? "Let me see if it's on the streaming service. I'm not sure my tv has the connector in the back for your ancient artifact." He used the remote to click to the search menu and found the movie, alongside the newer version. "You sure you don't want to watch this one?"

Summer called his bluff. "Sure. We can watch it after this one, then compare and contrast the two."

He clicked on the Colin Firth version. "Fine, we'll watch this one."

A little while into the movie, Summer pointed at the screen. "See? Doesn't Isaac remind you of Mr. Bingley?"

He could see it as soon as she said it. "They do kind of look alike."

"Right? I knew I wasn't imagining it. They're both fair with light, curly hair and that sort of approachable demeanor."

"And they're both filthy rich."

"That too. And Jane is quiet and reserved, just like Jillian. Although I think Jillian looks more like Rosamund Pike."

"Who?"

"She played Jane in the Keira Knightly version." She nudged his side. "You might not have noticed her."

He thought about it for a moment. "Was she also in *Gone Girl*?"

"Yes, that's her."

"That's funny, because I remember when I saw that movie I thought she looked a lot like Jillian." A few minutes later, he asked, "How'd you make out with your parents and the events?"

Summer grabbed the remote and paused the movie, then turned to prop her elbow on the back of the couch and face him. "It went really well, actually. I mentioned it to Mom and she said we have hosted a few bridal showers, but honestly, nobody thinks of us for anything other than weddings. Then she brought it up all on her own that maybe we should change the business name from Willow Creek Weddings to Willow Creek Events."

"What did your dad think of that?"

She made a horrified grimace. "That's what he thought of it. I'm pretty sure he hates the idea, but Nana loved it. I'm kind of stepping back and letting them hash it out. I'll wait a few days and toss out the idea of Willow Creek Weddings and Events. Ultimately, it's the marketing and not the name that matters."

"True."

"Even Dad was fairly receptive to holding a vendor event. You were right. Almost all the venues around us are doing similar things. I talked to Vanessa over at Spicy Cider. She said they've basically headlined a ton of these events, usually partnering with a few wineries. She gave me the number for a lady who organizes these events. Obviously I can figure it out, but it's so important to give people what they're expecting and not just what I think they should want."

"That sounds promising." He was glad to hear some excitement in her voice, as opposed to the resignation and defeat he'd been hearing.

"And I heard back from Isaac. We got approved for a grant that will cover a new computer and, thank goodness, a new chair. I just had to sign a super simple contract that said this is what we're spending the money on, I promise to provide the receipts, there is no obligation to repay this grant unless we don't provide the receipt, blah blah blah. He said we should have the money by Tuesday or Wednesday, which means I can go chair and laptop shopping."

"That's great."

"I'm thrilled. It's not like it'll solve all our problems, but the laptop is a big deal. My personal one is old, too, and I'll need it for myself when I find a place."

"Have you had much luck finding anything?"

"Not really, but I haven't had much time to look."

"Check the old schoolhouse. They had some vacancies last month when we were there doing some work."

"Is that the place out by the grocery store?"

"Yup."

She tapped her temple. "Mental note made."

"Speaking of made, I'm getting hungry. Since we're paused, I think I'll make those wings."

"And I think I'll take a bathroom break."

Ben went into the kitchen and started the air fryer. It was nice having Summer here. Just... being here. Watching movies, talking, eating. It tugged at his heart a little, when he could easily see a future just like this. The problem was that he had no clue how to make her stop seeing him as an extra brother. Assuming she did. He frowned a little. Was it possible that she didn't see him that way? He thought back over their recent interactions. She treated him like a friend. Hmm. That had to be an easier obstacle to overcome, didn't it?

He was lost in his thoughts, staring mindlessly at the little red dot on the air fryer that indicated the heat, when Summer tapped his arm and he nearly jumped out of his skin.

"My goodness, where were you?"

"Sorry, just pondering the dynamic between Mr. Collins and Lady Catherine."

"You were not. Come on, what's that lonely brain cell working so hard on?"

He decided it was now or never. He was going to say it. Just come out with it. Maybe she'd thought of him the same way, and they were both dancing around the subject. That was possible, right? Might as well get it out in the open. His throat felt tight and his stomach rolled anxiously. He cleared his throat. "Have you ever thought about the possibility of—"

The air fryer beeped, letting him know it had reached the correct temperature. He opened it and put the wings in, then set the timer.

"Thought about what?" She leaned against the counter and looked up at him curiously.

"Um, food trucks. Have you thought of having food trucks at the vendor thing?" No way could he muster that much courage again. He wasn't sure if he should be kicking himself for chickening out or high fiving himself for avoiding certain disaster.

"Oooh, that's a fantastic idea. See? I don't keep you around just because you're pretty." She poked her elbow into his side and chuckled.

He managed a laugh. "I *am* pretty, though."

"Eh, you're not hideous."

"That makes one of us." He sprinted to the other side of the island.

"Hey!" Summer whipped a potholder at him.

He caught it easily and threw it back. She deflected and knocked it to the floor.

"You're not gonna leave that on the floor are you?" He said as he laughed.

"Uuuhhh, yeah, I'm not picking it up."

"Yes you are."

"Pffft. Make me."

He was off like a shot, rounding the island. He grabbed Summer around her waist and lifted her off the ground. She squealed and giggled and swatted his back. "Put me down!"

"Not until you promise to pick up the potholder."

"Never!"

The air fryer beeped and flashed a message to flip the food. "Put me down."

"Nope. Stay still so I can flip these." He held her across his shoulder with one arm while she half-heartedly squirmed. "Careful, I don't want you to bump the fryer."

She stilled. "You are in so much trouble. As soon as I get down, I'm going all Apollo Creed on that pretty face of yours."

He flipped the last wing and closed the fryer. "You're awful mouthy for someone suspended in midair."

"You can't hold me forever, Ben."

He begged to differ. One word from her, and he certainly could.

Chapter Eighteen

Summer gripped the back of Ben's shirt as he started walking. "Where are you going? Put me down, you neanderthal!"

"I can't. I fear for my safety."

She waited until they were on the carpet of the living room, then jerked to the side.

He was ready for it and easily held her around the waist and swung her down so her feet dangled several inches above the floor. "Are you going to pick up the potholder?"

"Absolutely not."

"Then you're stuck."

"Ben!"

"Summer."

"Let me go this instant!"

"Nah." He sat on the couch pulling her with him. She landed on his lap and immediately took advantage of the change in position. She hooked one leg over his arm and twisted around, pushing back away from him.

He caught her off guard by letting go, but the second she tried to stand he had his arms around her waist again and pulled her against him. The laughter faded from both of them.

Breathing hard, her face was an inch from his. She knew she should pull back, but she didn't want to. In that moment, she wanted to press her lips to his and see what it would be like to kiss him. And if she wasn't mistaken, it seemed an awful lot like he might be having the same thought.

The air fryer's beep was like a glass of cold water. Summer pushed back. This time, he let her go. While he went to tend to the wings, she went to the bathroom to take a few deep breaths and straighten her shirt. What the heck just happened?

She went to the kitchen and Ben handed her a plate with that lopsided half-smile of his. "Ranch?"

"Of course. Who eats wings with no ranch?"

"Psychopaths, that's who."

She relaxed, glad they were back to their normal back and forth instead of... whatever that was. "What about people who use bleu cheese?"

"Low level psychopaths, because who eats mold on purpose?"

"Why are they only low level then?"

"Because it's still basically ranch."

"Moldy ranch."

"Exactly." He took the dressing bottle she held out and squirted a puddle on his plate.

They took their wings back to the living room and sat on the couch.

"Need a refill?" Ben asked, picking his own glass up from the coffee table.

"Yes, please." Summer handed him her glass.

A couple minutes later, he came back with two glasses of soda and a roll of paper towels.

Ben turned the movie back on and Summer put their earlier interaction completely out of her mind as Colin Firth climbed out of the pond, his legendary white shirt sticking to his handsome chest.

Ben nudged her with his elbow. "I guess I know why this is your favorite version."

She gave a guilty snicker. "That's part of it."

They finished their wings and polished off a bag of chips.

At one scene, Ben's lip curled up in disgust. "That Wickham guy's such a creep. Isn't Lydia only fifteen?"

"Yup."

A while later, Summer wiped tears from her eyes as Jane and Bingley and Lizzie and Darcy got into their carriages to ride off into their happily ever afters. She sniffled. "Well? What did you think?"

Ben stretched his back and shrugged one shoulder. "It wasn't bad."

Summer smacked his arm with the little throw pillow. "'Wasn't bad?' It's only one of the most incredible cinematic masterpieces ever and you say it wasn't bad?"

He grabbed the pillow and tossed it against her leg. "*Pirates of the Caribbean* is a cinematic masterpiece. Or even *Titanic*. This was okay."

She laughed. "Again with Keira Knightley? I guess I don't have to ask who your celebrity crush is."

He pointed to the tv. "You're one to talk. We just spent five hours watching your celebrity crush."

"I suppose I can't deny that."

"Next weekend we'll watch *Pirates*."

"And *Titanic*."

He grinned. "We can do surf and turf. Have a whole ocean theme."

"Oooh, shrimp cocktail."

"Lobster mac and cheese."

"Yes. And I'll get some of those Red Lobster cheddar bay biscuits."

"Red Lobster is an hour away."

Summer shook her head. "They have them in the grocery store."

"Really?"

"Yup. They're pretty close to the original, too." She took her dirty dishes to the kitchen. "You want these in the sink or the dishwasher?"

"Sink. I just ran the dishwasher and haven't put the clean stuff away."

She got her tote bag and went to the door to slip her shoes on.

Ben said, "I had fun."

"Me, too."

"Let me know when you get your computer. I can get Jeff to help if you need."

"I should be able to handle it, but if I get stuck I'll give you a call." She pulled the door open and went out to the front porch.

"Let me know for sure about next weekend. I know you're busy."

Summer appreciated that he was giving her an out, but she didn't need it. "Nope, we're good. It's a date."

He blinked a few times.

Uh oh. Why did she call it a date? And why did he look stunned that she had? Before she could kick herself for using those particular words, she said, "Bye!" and hustled to the car.

"What the heck happened there?" she asked the interior of her car.

It didn't have an answer, so she cranked up the radio and sang along. She was no closer to making sense of the situation fifteen minutes later when she pulled into the driveway and parked the car. Her plan was to go into the house and go straight upstairs, but that was immediately derailed by Gavin calling out from the kitchen, "Sum! Where you been?"

She set her tote bag on the step to carry upstairs, then trudged into the kitchen. "I was at Ben's. We were having a philosophical discussion on the classicalness of *Rocky* vs *Pride and Prejudice*."

He made a face.

Nana narrowed her eyes. "What else?"

"What do you mean?" Her face heated as everyone's attention directed at her.

Mack and Andi looked at each other and back to Summer.

"I mean did you guys fool around?"

"Nana!"

Nana just shrugged. "I'm just saying it would be about time."

"What?" Now her face was full-on burning. She sent Gavin a desperate "help me out here" look, which he ignored.

Jillian rolled her eyes. "Oh, please. Like Ben hasn't been coming over ten times a week just to see you. Up until you got home he'd stop by once or twice a month."

Gavin shook his head. "Hey, now. He's got a business to run."

"I highly doubt chasing after Summer is part of his business."

Summer jumped in. "Nobody's chasing anybody. Ben and I are friends."

"Must be nice. Have 'friend' Ben over here and 'friend' Isaac Frazier over here." She made air quotes every time she said "friend."

Now Summer was confused. "Isaac? What are you talking about?"

"He keeps coming here to see you."

Andi frowned. "He's been here on business."

"Allegedly. It makes more sense to go from a rich celebrity chef to a rich investment banker than to downgrade to a handyman."

"Hey! They're no better than Ben." Gavin cautioned her.

Summer was no longer embarrassed. She was getting mad. "You're so ridiculous. First of all, Ben's not a downgrade from Michael Mastriano by any stretch, and Isaac and I aren't friends. It's purely business."

"For now," Jillian scoffed.

"What is your problem?"

"Girls," Andi started.

"My problem is you, waltzing back in to be the center of attention and collect men like some people collect baseball cards with your flashy, fake, over-the-top personality and batting your eyelashes like you do."

"Hey, maybe I'll try being bitter and critical and judgmental since it's clearly working well for you."

"Summer!" Nana scolded.

"Really? I didn't hear you say 'Jillian!' when she was being nasty to me two seconds ago. At least pretend not to play favorites, please."

Nana pressed her lips together disapprovingly.

Summer wasn't sure when the evening had gone off the rails, but she was done with it. She wanted to hang onto the feeling of having a great day. No arguing, no drama, just food, movies, and fun. She decided to go to the office for a while and maybe go online to shop for a new computer.

She was halfway across the wet grass when Gavin said, "Hey, wait up."

He caught up to her and they walked to The Shoppes together. He held the door open. "What are you doing?"

"I guess I'll do some paperwork or look at computers online."

"Nah. Come have some cake instead."

It wasn't hard to convince her. She followed him into the bakery. "Smells good."

"I had a tasting this afternoon so I baked a fresh coconut lime cake."

"Mmm, please tell me you have some left."

"Have a seat." He grinned and went into the back as she sat at the table he used for clients.

A few minutes later, he came back with a platter full of a dozen tasting-sized samples of cake, two forks, and a pitcher of ice water.

Summer jumped up and got two plastic cups from the counter.

"Okay, sir, I'd like a cake with a layer of this," she pointed," this, this, this, this, this, this, maybe some of this, definitely some of this, and this. I can probably live without this or this."

He laughed. "I knew you'd pass on those."

She eyed the chocolate cakes. "They look too rich."

"They are. So take a little taste of those first and get it over with."

She took a small sliver of the dark chocolate cake with the dark chocolate frosting. "Very moist. I can see why people would like it, but it's super rich. Not for me."

Gavin took a forkful of the cake. "Sum, you should go easier on Jilly."

She set her fork down and sat back. "Don't start, Gav. You were right there. I did nothing. She's the one who went off and started insinuating things about me. She's no better than Nina Hardwick, and I'm not going to sit here and listen to how I need to let poor, poor Jillian say whatever she wants and never defend myself in case it hurts her feelings. Forget that."

He sighed.

She tried another angle. "If anybody else in the world said those exact words to me, would you be telling me to go easy on them?"

"Probably not," he conceded.

"I've got big shoulders, Gav. But I can only take so much for so long."

"I know."

"I realize she's not thrilled about me being back home. Newsflash, neither am I. I was literally getting death threats and had my car vandalized, and she can't extend a tiny bit of grace and not make nasty comments every chance she gets? Sorry, I'm not getting on the poor Jillian train. I've *been* holding back, and if she can't take it down a notch, I can stop being nice." She started at Gavin until he looked at her. "You know it's the truth. I don't deserve it, and I'm not going to keep taking it."

"I probably shouldn't tell you this."

She forced out an annoyed huff, preparing herself for another reason for Jillian to act like a spoiled brat.

"I think she's got a crush on Isaac Frazier."

Summer stabbed her fork into the second dark chocolate cake. "What, exactly, does that have to do with me?"

"He's been here a bunch, talking to you, and—"

Summer cut him off. "He's also met with Mom twice. Does that mean she's after him, too? Using her cougarly wiles to seduce him into giving us grant money? Give. Me. A. Break." She rolled her eyes so hard she thought they might get stuck.

"I'm just telling you what I know. You know how it is. It's harder for her to talk to people."

"I won't apologize for being outgoing and having an easier time dealing with people any more than I would apologize for having dark hair and blue eyes." She ate the next bite of cake. "I like this one much better."

"It's less dense, so the flavor isn't quite as intense as the first one."

"I don't get it. You and I are so similar, but she loves you to pieces. You're yin and yang. Her and I are oil and water. I really resent the idea that I'm flirting with Isaac just because I'm nice to him. Believe me, I have zero interest in him. He's so not my type."

"I know. I told her as much."

"Well, next time tell her it's really misogynistic and gross to assume I can't be a professional businesswoman without schtupping every man I deal with."

He snickered. "I think I'll leave that part out."

"What's this one?"

"Orange cake with a cream cheese drizzle."

She sniffed the bite on her fork. "It smells amazing."

"Let's get back to Ben. You were over there all day talking about movies?"

"Watching the movies. And eating. Did you know his nachos are the absolute bomb?"

"Yup. He brought them to the Super Bowl party last year."

"Nice. Next week we're doing an ocean theme. He's making lobster mac and cheese."

Gavin carefully asked, "What's going on with you two?"

"I don't know," Summer admitted. "Everything was totally normal until we were getting wings, and then we were kind of playing around in the kitchen and blah, blah, blah, we were on the couch, and I thought for a minute that I was going to kiss him. But that's crazy. It's *Ben*."

Gavin shrugged. "He probably wanted to."

"Really? You think so?"

"Summer, you can't be that dense. He's been in love with

you since the eighth grade when he realized you were an actual girl."

Apparently she could be that dense. She remembered that exact moment Gavin was talking about. She'd been in ninth grade and getting ready for the freshman dance. When she came down the stairs in her fancy dress, Ben's eyes had gotten huge and he'd said, "You have *boobs.*"

Andi had smacked the back of his head as Gavin yelled, "EEEWWWW!"

Summer had promptly forgotten the whole thing because Ben was her annoying little brother's annoying little friend.

She wracked her brain trying to find other clues but came up empty. He was *Ben.* He'd always just been Ben. Her brother's best friend. "Why didn't he ever say anything, then?"

"Beats me."

"This orange cake is a keeper."

"Try this one." He pointed to a yellow cake with white frosting.

She took a bite and savored the taste. "Mmmm, lemon and... what is that? Blueberry?"

"Yup."

"Nice. I like that a lot."

Gavin set his fork down. "What are you going to do about Ben?"

It was the million dollar question, wasn't it? They were friends. She trusted him and enjoyed spending time with him. Was it heading to something more than that? Did she *want* it to? "I have no idea."

Chapter Nineteen

Sunday morning brought a cold drizzle, which perfectly matched Ben's mood. He spent the night tossing and turning, trying to analyze Saturday. He knew if the air fryer hadn't gone off, he would have kissed Summer. And he was pretty sure she would have let him. Then they both pretended nothing happened, but when she left and said it was a date… It was driving him bananas overthinking what she meant. Was she just saying words, or did she really mean date?

He was pondering her tone of voice as he polished off a bowl of Cheerios over the sink and debated cancelling his driving range meetup with Gavin. Gavin's advice for years – decades, in fact – had been to forget about Summer and move on, because she was gone and never coming back to Willow Creek.

Turned out she had come back, but for how long? Once the Chicago mess blew over, would she head back to Chicago? Maybe New York? LA?

This was one of those situations where it wasn't great to be best friends with the brother of the woman he had feelings for because he knew too much about both sides.

In the end, he decided to keep their long-standing driving range appointment, mainly because he wanted to whack some golf balls into oblivion.

He met Gavin in the parking lot of the golf course at a quarter to eleven. They got their clubs and buckets of golf balls and headed up the concrete stairs to the second story of the driving range with barely a word between them. They picked two squares of artificial green turf beside each other.

"How'd movie day go yesterday?"

Apparently they were getting straight to it. Ben set a ball on the tee and inched his feet until he was in the stance he wanted. "It was good." Ben whacked his ball without saying more, knowing Gavin wouldn't be able to keep quiet long if he had something on his mind.

"Summer seemed to have a pretty good time."

"Good."

Gavin hit his ball. They watched it sail high and drop at the twenty-yard marker. "Said you made her watch *Rocky*."

"I didn't exactly make her. If anyone was made to do anything, it was Summer who made me sit through five hours of Mr. Darcy."

Gavin chuckled and set another ball. "Sounds like torture. Anything interesting happen besides the movies?"

Ben said mildly, "I'm golfing but I think you're fishing."

Gavin whacked his ball a little short of three hundred yards. "I'm just concerned."

"About what?" Ben hit his ball to the two-hundred-yard sign.

"About her. You. Mostly you."

That piqued his interest. "Why? What did she say?"

Gavin set his next ball. "Said she almost kissed you."

Ben swung wide left of his ball. "She did?" *That* was an

interesting development. He thought he'd been the one to almost kiss her.

"Is that what happened?"

Ben hit his ball but lost sight of it against the backdrop of the cloudy sky. He had no idea where it ended up. "Yeah, sort of. We were playing around and I picked her up and carried her into the living room and she ended up on my lap. And then it got real serious for a second and I thought it was me that almost kissed her, and then the air fryer went off and wrecked the moment."

"What happened after that?" Gavin hit his next ball.

Voices floated up from the lower deck as the driving range got busier.

"We ate wings and watched the rest of the movie, and both of us acted like nothing happened."

"Something definitely happened. You and Summer need to have a conversation."

"Why do you sound like that?"

"I'm worried. You're my best friend. Summer's my sister. If this doesn't work out…"

Ben planted his club onto the floor and looked directly at his best friend. "Hold up, Gav. There's nothing to work out or not work out. We just watched a movie."

Gavin pointed out, "And you're watching more movies this weekend."

That answered that, didn't it? She must actually be planning for them to get together. He wasn't sure if that made things more or less clear. "It's not a big deal." His words didn't convince himself, so he knew Gavin wasn't buying it.

Gavin said nothing, but gave a little noncommittal grunt.

He turned back to his tee and set a ball. "Trying not to get my hopes up over one afternoon of movies and something that might have happened but never did. Besides, she just got out of a toxic relationship not even a month ago."

"That relationship wasn't serious at all. She wasn't invested."

"Yeah, well…" He trailed off, unsure about the direction this conversation was going. So he hit his ball and changed the subject altogether. "Mom said your new lemon cake was better than the old recipe."

Like he usually did, Gavin rolled with the clear sign Ben was done with this subject for now. "Good. That's what she told me, but I'm never sure if she's just being polite."

"Mom? Please. She's not going to lie to save your feelings. If she didn't like it, she would have told you."

"That's probably true."

They hit the rest of their balls in companionable silence. Ben scooped up his empty basket and waited for Gavin to hit his last ball. "Lunch in the clubhouse?"

"Heck, yeah."

As they returned their clubs and ball buckets to the station, Gavin said, "You know, I asked Summer if there might be something between you two."

Ben slid his club into its slot. "Oh?"

Gavin shrugged. "She didn't say no."

Chapter Twenty

On Wednesday, Summer met the UPS driver at the front door and lugged the heavy box containing her new chair up the stairs to the office. It took half an hour and a handful of frustrated words to get the holes lined up so she could get the screws in and tight.

Finally she was able to set it upright and slide her brightly colored polka dot cover over the faux leather. Who knew they made slipcovers for office chairs? Best part was that they were cheap, so she could change it out every season if she wanted to.

She sat down in the chair and tested it out. She even spun around and it didn't try to fling her off. Perfect.

Her phone vibrated with an incoming call from a familiar number she hadn't heard from in a long while. She answered with an excited, "Ashley! I haven't talked to you in ages." Her friend was also a wedding planner in a neighboring town.

"Hey! I heard you were home and I hate to ask for a favor before we even catch up, but I'm desperate."

"Oh no, what's up?"

"I have a bride whose venue canceled on her. I was crossing

my fingers and hoping you might be able to squeeze in a bridal shower Friday night."

Summer sat upright. "Friday? *This* Friday? The day after tomorrow?"

"Yeah. I know. It's so last minute and I've called everywhere I could think of." Her voice hitched on the last words.

"What do you need? I don't know if we can arrange a caterer or anything with this short notice." A surge of sympathy made her want to help. She'd had venues cancel last minute a time or two, and it was no fun rearranging everything in a panic.

"No, no, just the space. We have caterer, decorations, everything. We'd just need tables and chairs and tables for the caterer to set up the buffet. Maybe background music."

"How many people?" Summer tapped her pen on the desk, considering what they'd need to do in a short amount of time.

"About thirty, thirty-five."

Summer thought over the logistics. She could set them up in Creekside Hall. They'd just need to get all those burned out lightbulbs replaced, which shouldn't be a problem since they had them, they just hadn't swapped them out. Otherwise the building was ready to go. "Do you want the fabric walls set up so it's not a wide open space?"

"That would be amazing."

"Email me all the details, with *everything* you need and I'll go see if we can staff the event. Right now it's a tentative yes, and for such short notice we'll collect the fee up front with the contract."

"No problem." She lowered her voice. "Honestly, I'd tack on a convenience fee. These people have money to burn. They're not even asking the other venue for their deposit back."

"Why'd the venue cancel?" A red flag went up in her mind.

There was a long pause. "Family stuff?"

The red flag waved. "You're not sending me a bridezilla, are you?"

Ashley's response was immediate. "I promise, no bridezilla. This bride is the sweetest person. Not an ounce of drama from her. She's been a dream to work with."

"Okay. Get me the details and I'll get the contract ready."

Summer's grabbed the walkie and spoke to her mom.

After that, Summer hustled over to Creekside Hall with her clipboard. She flipped the lights on and was mildly disappointed to see the lightbulbs hadn't replaced themselves.

Armed with sudden inspiration, she sketched a rough grid and numbered all the bulbs, then noted the ones that were out. That should make it easier to replace than flipping the switch on and off and on and off a million times.

Her dad and Gavin came in with the ladder.

"Your mom said fixing the lights just became top priority."

"True. Don't you be climbing on that ladder."

Mack waved a hand, dismissing her concerns. "I've got my babysitter."

Gavin just shook his head.

Summer checked her list. "Are the panels for the fabric walls still in this storage room, or were they moved over to the office?"

"I think they're still here," Mack answered.

She gave them the list of which bulbs were out and went to the storage room to find the flowy fabric panels that would be affixed to hidden clips in the rafters. The panels visually cut the room in half to make smaller events feel more intimate and cozy without sacrificing the aesthetic integrity of the room.

Amazingly, the fabric panels were right where they were supposed to be. Summer took it as a good omen for the event.

It was an even better omen when Ashley emailed her the

signed contract barely thirty minutes after receiving it, along with an electronic transfer for the full payment.

This was going to be a breeze.

Friday's hours flew like minutes. Summer checked, double checked, triple checked, and probably quadruple checked that everything in Creekside Hall was ready to go. She changed into her event uniform of black pants and a black shirt.

The caterer showed up at four thirty, right on time. "Hey, Summer, are we along this wall?"

"Hi, Calvin. You can set up over here any way you want. Do you need help bringing stuff in?"

"Nah, we got it."

They made some small talk while he set up his buffet warmers. Then he caught her off guard by saying, "I was a little surprised you agreed to take this event after Spicy Cider gave them the boot."

"Wait, what?" She leaned toward him to make sure she'd heard correctly.

He froze. "They were supposed to have this shower at Spicy Cider."

"Ashley just told me the venue canceled for family reasons. I didn't know what venue. Is Vanessa okay?"

"Vanessa?" He looked confused, then caught on. He set his warmer down and turned to face her. "Vanessa's fine. And I'd have a few words with Ashley if I were you. Vanessa gave them the boot because this family is a bunch of drama llamas."

"She said the bride is wonderful. No drama at all."

"The bride? True enough. She's super nice. The bride's mother? Well, have you ever seen *Real Housewives*?"

"Please tell me you're kidding."

His grin turned serious. "For real, though, you might want to have some security. Just in case."

"You're making me nervous, Cal." Doubly nervous, because even though Calvin was a massive gossip, he wasn't one to make things up.

"Just saying, stay on your toes."

"Thanks for the heads up." She left him to set up and went to find Gavin.

She filled him in. "Do you think I should try to round up some help?"

"You've got enough going on. I'll call around, get a few guys to come over and look tough. It'll probably cost you a couple pizzas and a case of beer."

"Deal. Thank you."

While Gavin handled that, she hurried back to Creekside Hall to put the finishing touches on the tables.

Ashley arrived at ten after five. "Everything looks incredible." She leaned in for a quick side-hug.

Summer yanked her close. "Yeah, you forgot to mention the family problems with the venue were actually problems with this family."

She had the decency to look a little bit sorry. "I did it for the bride. She really is the sweetest person. And maybe getting booted from the venue last minute was a wakeup call and they'll behave."

Summer wasn't buying that line, not one little bit. "Sure. What kind of music do you want piped in?"

"The moms are kind of bougie, so how about some classical."

"You got it." She went to start the music and checked with Calvin again to make sure he and his staff didn't need anything.

The party was scheduled to start at six. At ten after, the

doors opened and the bride and her guests poured into the room.

"Oh, it's so pretty!" The petite blonde looked around with a big smile.

"Hi, you must be Trina. Congratulations." Summer gave her best customer service smile.

Trina shook her hand warmly as her party swarmed the room, depositing gifts on the gift table and finding their places at the tables.

As Calvin and his team served the meal, Summer popped into the side room where Gavin, Ben, and two other friends congregated, waiting.

"They seem like a pretty chill bunch," Ben said.

"Yeah, so far. Maybe it was all overstated."

Frank joked, "We still get pizza and beer, though, right?"

"Yes," she laughed. "You'll still get pizza and beer."

Her eyes caught Ben's and held for a beat. She hadn't seen him since Saturday.

That was entirely too long.

Chapter Twenty-One

The guys sat at the counter in the storage room, talking about random things in low voices. They took turns peeking in and checking on the group, which seemed to be nothing more than a group of women laughing and eating and having a good time.

Ben moved the door slightly and looked in just as the groom's mother accidentally bumped a glass and sent a river of red wine into the lap of the bride's mother.

The bride's mother jumped to her feet with a shriek.

Ben hissed to the guys, "Be ready."

They joined him in peering at the scene from behind the cracked-open door.

"Look what you did!"

The groom's mother didn't look particularly apologetic. "So what? That dress is hideous anyway."

Ben's jaw dropped. Yikes.

The bride's mother snatched her own glass from the table and yelled, "I'd like to make a toast! To you and your cheap, tacky wine ruining my beautiful dress the way your cheap, tacky son ruined my beautiful daughter!"

"You're the cheap, tacky one!"

The bride sat, her mouth hanging open as she looked back and forth between the two women like a tennis match.

"Cheers." The bride's mother put her glass to her lips, then instead, flicked her wrist and splashed the wine at the groom's mother.

"What are you doing? You lunatic!"

"Payback, you cow!"

The groom's mother, probably close to sixty years old, sprang across the table with impressive agility.

Plates and silverware clattered to the ground.

The bridal party hustled to grab the glassware out of harm's way.

"Stop it!" the bride yelled over and over.

By the time Ben and the guys made it across the room, the groom's mother had her hands around the bride's mother's neck.

Not to be outdone, the bride's mother yanked her opponent off the table and wrenched out of her grasp. The tablecloth and all the plates went with her. Uneaten food splashed and rolled and splattered and bounced everywhere.

All thirty of the ladies in attendance were on their feet, most of them moving away from the scene.

Both mothers went off balance, their arms cartwheeling. The bride's mother launched herself at the groom's mother and tackled her into the gift table. Carefully wrapped packages flew in every direction, torn and battered.

Ben grabbed the groom's mother as Gavin took hold of the bride's mother. He tried not to grab her too roughly because he didn't want to hurt her, but it was like baptizing a tiger. He had to tighten his grip to keep her from squirming away.

Both women kicked and swung at each other while exchanging loud curses and insults.

The groom's mother's fingers caught in the bride's mother's hair and pulled the long blonde curls right off her head. She cackled with glee as the bride's mother screamed and clutched the netted wig cap that held her gray locks in place.

Ben and Gavin both pulled backwards, dragging the women apart.

"I *told* my son he was marrying into crazy!"

"And I told my daughter she was marrying into trash!"

Summer was animatedly talking with the sobbing bride.

Ben hooked the groom's mother under the arms more securely and pulled her toward the door.

Gavin mirrored his actions, dragging the mother of the bride out the opposite door.

The women screamed obscenities at each other, even after they were out of each other's sight.

Ben caught a foot to the shin along the way. He grunted and struggled to keep his balance. Frank was beside him, getting the door. He hurried to close it behind them once they were outside. The groom's mother breathed hard from the exertion. She struggled out of Ben's grasp and stood, huffing and puffing as she smoothed the front of her dress.

"Ma'am, are you hurt?"

She glared. "That hag ripped my dress."

"Where are your shoes?"

"I kicked them off when she came at me."

Ben didn't waste any breath explaining that she was the one who had launched across the table.

"Well? Go get them. This concrete is freezing." She snapped her fingers inches from Frank's face. "Chop chop."

Frank was uncertain. "Uh, you want me to get them?" he asked Ben.

Ben sized her up. He was pretty sure he could grab her and

keep her in place if she tried to take off, which was unlikely since the object of her fury wasn't in view. "Yeah."

Frank asked, "What kind of shoes were you wearing?"

She threw him a withering glare. "Jimmy Choos."

He stared blankly. "Uhhh, what color?"

"Black, you dolt." She looked at Ben and shook her head. As if he'd understand, she motioned to her dress. "What color shoes *would* I be wearing with this?" She rolled her eyes for emphasis.

A few awkward minutes passed as they waited for Frank and the Jimmy Choos.

The groom's mother broke the silence with, "You saw that, right? Would your mother let you marry into a family like that? Ridiculous, all of them. Well, Trina's okay I guess, but you know what they say. You're not just marrying your partner. You're marrying the whole family. I don't want my precious son shackled to those nuts. I mean, come on." She shook the blonde wig for emphasis.

Ben managed a polite smile, but said nothing. He fully believed that she and the bride's mother were equally unhinged.

"Where is he with my shoes? I'm going back inside."

"Umm…" Ben couldn't think of a reason to make her stand outside in the cold in her bare feet since she'd calmed down considerably. "I'm going to have to ask you to behave."

She flashed him a charming smile. "Sure." There was a long pause. "As long as she does."

Ben opened the door and let her walk inside. He stayed close to her. The scene inside was still chaos. The bride's friends were picking up destroyed gifts. Summer, Jillian, Andi, and Mack were cleaning up the floor.

Over in the corner, the bride and another woman who looked to be around the same age were sitting close together.

The second woman was rubbing the bride's shoulder and speaking intently to her while the bride nodded.

A shrill voice split the air. "GIVE ME MY HAIR!"

The groom's mother waved the wig triumphantly. "Come and get it!"

Before Ben could move, the groom's mother spun around and ran out the door they'd just come in. He whipped back and reached, but the bride's mother darted just out of reach. He regretted letting his guard down.

He gave chase, bursting out the door behind them, with Gavin, Frank, and Dan right behind.

The bride's mother had longer legs, and almost caught up with the groom's mother halfway to the gazebo. The groom's mother took a sharp right and ran back toward the building.

The bride's mother pivoted quickly and reached out. She caught the groom's mother's dress.

They all heard the fabric tear.

"Oh, crap," Ben breathed and came to a stop. The other guys joined him, staring at the scene with no clue how to intervene.

The groom's mother screeched and whirled, smacking the bride's mother in the face with her own wig.

The women locked onto each other in a flurry of arms and legs and hair.

Gavin grunted. "We have to stop this, right?"

Ben nodded. "Yeah, I think we do."

The four men started forward.

The women lost their balance and fell over in a heap, swinging and kicking.

"Look out!" Ben yelled, but it was too late.

They rolled a little too far and plopped right into the creek. Both of them screamed and scrambled, thwarting each other's efforts to get out of the cold water.

Dan muttered, "This is gonna cost more than a pizza."

They reached the bank. Ben and Frank grabbed the groom's mother's arms and pulled her up the short bank. Gavin and Dan pulled the bride's mother up.

Ben watched Summer's jaw drop as the two mothers, dripping wet and still feral, were escorted back into the building.

She shook her head. "We're going to have to ask you to leave."

The bride stood and squared her shoulders. "Mom, Gloria, you're no longer welcome to the wedding. Neither of you can come."

The bride's mother glared at her nemesis. "Now look what you've done!"

Gavin caught her as she lunged. Ben stepped in front of Gloria.

Summer stalked over and gave them both a hard glare. "If you can't see yourselves out without a fuss, I'll call the police to assist."

One of the younger women came over to take custody of Gloria. She gripped her upper arm. "Let's go."

"I need my shoes. And my purse."

Ashley dug through a pile of debris and came over with Gloria's things.

Gloria lifted her chin and walked toward the door as regally as one could with a shredded dress and twigs in one's dripping wet hair.

Two firemen burst through the door. One of them carried a helmet and the other had a... boombox. "Oh, yeeeeeaaaaah, it sure is hot in here!" He called out, "Let's get this party started!" and pressed a button. Thumping music blasted from the speaker.

"Who's the lucky lady?" the other one asked as he ripped

his yellow jacket open and tossed it aside, revealing suspenders over oily abs.

Summer sliced her hand back and forth across her throat. "Nope, nope, nope, turn it off."

The firemen exchanged a look and stopped dancing.

Summer gestured to the boombox until he got the hint and turned it off. "Sorry, gentlemen, we had to shut the party down early."

From the far corner of the room, the bride burst out laughing. A handful of women, Ben assumed her bridal party, were with her and started laughing as well. The awkward tension over the event broke.

Ben found Summer and gave a one-shouldered shrug to ask her what to do. She jabbed her thumb toward the exit, so he nudged Frank and they escorted Gloria out. The woman who'd grabbed her arm followed them out, apologizing on Gloria's behalf.

They'd secured Gloria in the car when Gavin and Dan came out flanking the bride's mother who looked none too pleased to be leaving.

As a precaution, they waited until Gloria was gone and out of sight before allowing the bride's mother to leave.

They stood together, watching the taillights of her car.

"I'm asking for hazard pay on top of the pizza," Dan joked.

Frank snickered. "What kind of hazard pay?"

"Breadsticks. And one of those cookie pizza dessert things."

"And a two-liter bottle of soda," Ben added.

They went back inside.

The party had mostly broken up. The bride, Ashley, and three other women remained.

The firemen were gone.

Calvin and his crew boxed up the leftovers and got out of Dodge as soon as the melee started.

Summer and Andi folded the linens and stacked them while Mack mopped the floor.

Ashley, the wedding planner with questionable judgment, was carefully sorting the gifts into piles of damaged and not damaged.

Gavin offered, "We can help take those out to the car if you want."

"That'd be great, thanks."

Ben dutifully took an armload of gifts that crunched and jangled as he walked. "What a shame," he muttered to Dan. "Hopefully they decide to run away and elope."

"And live in Australia," Dan added.

"You're not kidding."

When everyone from the party was gone, Summer thanked the guys profusely. "I can't even imagine how that would have gone if you weren't here. I'll have to call Calvin and thank him for the heads up." She pulled money out of her pocket and handed it to Frank. "Pizza and beer."

"And breadsticks?" Dan asked.

She laughed. "And breadsticks. And a generous tip. Seriously. Thank you all so much."

Something in her forced laugh caught his attention. He watched her walk to the storage room. "I'll meet up with you guys at Slices."

Gavin hesitated, but headed out with Frank and Dan.

Ben went to the storage room but didn't see Summer. He walked around the island and found her sitting on the floor behind a rack of folding chairs. "You okay?"

She leaned her head back against the wall. "Is everybody gone?"

"Yeah." He reached over and pushed the door shut just in case, then sat down facing her. "What's up?"

"I'm just annoyed. Or something. I'm not even sure. This

was a hot mess, and Dad decided it was a good time to corner me to say it's a horrible idea to have non-wedding events and this is the perfect example."

Ben frowned. "That makes no sense. These women would have done the same thing at a wedding reception, with a bigger audience, more food, more damage, and it would have been a lot harder to get under control."

"That's what Mom and I said." She sighed. "I mean, even if he had a point, was now really the time to say something?"

"Definitely not."

"I'm tired. And that makes everything a million times worse."

"It's been a crazy day."

She gave him a small smile. "At least tomorrow I can relax."

His spirits soared with the realization she viewed spending the day with him as something to look forward to. "Did you make your cheddar bay biscuits?"

"Nope, I'll do it in the morning." She yawned. "You better go find the boys. They won't save any pizza for you."

"True." He got up and held his hands down to help her up.

When she was on her feet, he pulled her to him for a hug. "You did a great job tonight, Sum. Do you have food?"

"Oh, yeah. I told Ashley I was keeping some of Cal's left-overs in exchange for not strangling her."

He laughed. "Good trade."

They walked out into the main ballroom. It looked like nothing had ever happened.

"I'll see you tomorrow," he said.

"Can't wait."

He couldn't wait, either.

Chapter Twenty-Two

Ben wasn't kidding. Summer couldn't believe his surf and turf spread. "You really went all out." She put her warm, fresh-from-the-oven cheddar bay biscuits on the counter next to a tray of seared steak tips.

"It was fun. I like cooking, but it always seems kind of silly to do anything fancy when it's just for myself. Stand back." He slipped his hands into oven mitts and pulled the door open. A cloud of delicious heat escaped as he pulled a casserole dish out.

"Is that the mac and cheese?"

"Yes, ma'am." He pulled the foil off the dish and they both inhaled.

"That smells amazing." Beyond amazing, really. It was macaroni and cheese perfection from what she could tell so far.

"It has five kinds of cheese."

She joked, "That you shredded by hand."

"I did."

"You're joking."

He looked at her intently. "I never joke about cheese."

"Five kinds? Cheddar, mozzarella, parmesan?" she guessed.

"Yes to the cheddar." He ticked the cheeses off on his fingers. "Gruyere, fontina, Monterey Jack, and Romano."

"Wow. Bougie cheeses."

"There's a plate of appetizers in the fridge. Top shelf."

Summer was shocked at how much effort he'd put into this. She went to the fridge and got out a foil-covered plate. "What's this?"

"Take a look."

She lifted the foil. "You're kidding. These belong on a magazine cover."

Thin slices of cucumber were topped with dollops of a crabmeat mixture, with thin curls of bell pepper on top for garnish.

Ben grinned. "I also made a crab dip, but I figured we could have that between movies."

"I'm still going to be stuffed between movies."

He moved behind her to grab something from the island and lightly rested his hand on her hip as he did so.

She stayed still, probably reading way too much into the casual gesture. Or, more accurately, reading too much into the fact that she wouldn't mind if his hand stayed right there. "I feel like a slacker with just biscuits and shrimp cocktail. I didn't even make that myself." She said as she opened the jar of cocktail sauce.

"You didn't need to bring anything at all." He put a lobster tail on a plate.

"Are you kidding me? You even have ramekins with melted butter?"

"Not just butter. Garlic butter with fresh herbs."

"Fresh?"

He laughed. "Okay, I made that one up. The herbs are courtesy of McCormick." He pointed to the bottle with the glass bottle with the black grinder lid.

"So you did grind them yourself."

"Technically, I suppose."

"Showoff."

He grinned. "Check this out." He put two cookie sheets on the counter. On one, he put a ramekin of his melted butter, a small plate with the cold appetizers, and a dinner plate with the hot food. "Dinner trays."

"You're a genius." Summer put her food on the other cookie sheet.

They carried their makeshift trays to the living room. Ben set his down on the coffee table and said, "I'll get the drinks."

Summer sat down and grabbed the remote. She navigated to the first *Pirates of the Caribbean* movie while Ben rattled around in the kitchen.

He came back carefully carrying two glasses of iced tea and a plastic pitcher filled with the same. He sat down beside her and looked over their trays. "Do we need anything else?"

Summer glanced over her tray. "Nope, looks like we got it all. The trays make it feel like we're back in school."

"I don't remember ever getting lobster at school."

She laughed. "I think fish sticks were probably as close as it got."

"I loved those fish sticks. Mmm. Fish sticks and tater tots."

"Was that your favorite school lunch?"

He dug into his mac and cheese. "It was in the top five. Spaghetti day was always good, too. Pizza for sure."

"Definitely the pizza. Those rectangles with one sad little pepperoni. I always ate the whole way around it so I could have the pepperoni on the last bite."

"I always ate the pepperoni first."

Summer popped one of the steak tips into her mouth. "This is so good. Did you marinate them?"

"Nope, just sautéed in the garlic herb butter. Same as that." He pointed to the ramekin.

"Really? It's so good."

"Better than school pizza?"

She put her fingers to her lips to cover her mouth as she laughed. "Definitely. But I'm not sure it beats vegetable soup day."

He frowned at her. "Vegetable soup day? *That's* your favorite?"

She nodded enthusiastically and swallowed the steak. "Yep. Vegetable soup, Lebanon bologna sandwich, and the best part – the sticky bun." She could almost smell the sticky sweetness of it from her memories.

"Oooohhh, I forgot about those."

"I'd always dip my sandwich in the soup, which I still like to do, by the way, and then eat that amazing, huge, delicious sticky bun that was as big as your head." She held her hands up to demonstrate. "They don't make them like that anymore."

"They do, actually."

"Okay, but they probably won't let me in to eat with a bunch of kids."

"You haven't heard of Mr. Sticky's?"

"Nope." Was he making a joke?

A slow smile spread across his face. "I think I just figured out what we're doing next Saturday. I'll give up my movie pick. We'll go to Mr. Sticky's and eat sticky buns while we watch whatever movie you want."

"Where is it?"

"Carlisle Pike."

"Are you teasing me?"

He pressed a hand to his heart. "I would never."

"It's a real place?"

"It's a real place. They've been to the fair with their food truck. They do fundraiser stuff with the schools, too."

"No kidding." She grabbed her phone from her pocket and looked them up. Yup, totally real. She scrolled through the pictures on their website. "These look amazing."

"I'm telling you, they're the best."

Summer put her phone away and took a bite of mac and cheese. She pointed at it with her fork. "No, *this* is the best. Oh, my goodness, Ben, this is incredible. You should have been a chef."

He blushed a little at the praise. To deflect, he pressed the play button on the remote.

Will Turner had barely sprung Jack Sparrow from jail to go rescue Elizabeth Swann when Summer's eyes started to get heavy. All the food settled pleasantly in her belly.

"You look like you're about to fall asleep," Ben said quietly.

"I can't, though. My feet are too cold."

He got off the couch and went upstairs. A few minutes later, he was back with a fuzzy blanket and a plush throw pillow shaped like a penguin.

She laughed as she took it from him. "Do you sleep with this?"

"Ha, ha. It was in the closet. Kyler gave it to me for Christmas a couple years ago."

"Why?"

"Jenna said they'd just done a penguin craft in school, and then he watched a documentary on penguins, so everybody got penguin gifts that year."

"That's adorable." She fluffed the penguin against the arm of the couch and covered her legs with the blanket. She curled up on her side and watched the movie.

Ben slid a hand under the blanket and tickled her foot. "No

wonder your feet are cold in these thin socks. What's even the point?"

"So my Chucks don't get stinky."

"You can wear heavier socks in your Chucks."

"Yeah but then you see them. These are no-show."

"They're no-point."

"Shhh, I like this scene."

Ben snorted. "Orlando Bloom in a wet shirt?"

She poked his side with her toe. "You jealous?"

He grabbed her foot and pulled it onto his lap. His hands were warm as they kneaded her foot.

She sighed. "The nail girl I went to in Chicago did the most amazing foot massages. I think I miss her more than anything else."

"More than Chicago deep dish?"

"Hmmm. Right now? Yes. But I'm stuffed to the gills." She snickered at her own joke. "See what I did there? Gills?"

He groaned. "Yeah, yeah, I see what you did there."

The movie drew their attention, so they went quiet for a long while until the credits rolled.

Summer couldn't believe she'd stayed awake the whole time. "Do you have more of the cucumber things? Those were awesome."

"Yep, and I have the crab dip and tortilla chips." He said, "Do you want to set up *Titanic* and I'll bring the food in?"

Summer reluctantly pulled her feet off his lap so he could stand up. "Actually, do you care if we just watch the second *Pirates* movie? I don't think I'm in the mood for Jack and Rose."

"Like I'm going to turn down another two hours of Keira Knightley," he joked as he headed for the kitchen.

"I think you mean two hours of Orlando Bloom. And Johnny Depp."

"Whatever *floats your boat*," he called from the kitchen.

"I see what you did there," she yelled back. She sat up and fiddled with the remote to queue up the next movie. Then she sat cross-legged and adjusted the blanket so she was nice and cozy.

Ben had taken their trays of dirty dishes with him, and brought back one tray with a bowl of crab dip, a bag of tortilla chips, and a plate of the cucumber slices with crab meat.

"Did I mention how awesome you are? This is fantastic," she said, popping a cucumber in her mouth with one hand as she scooped crab dip with a tortilla with her other.

"I did rather outdid myself, didn't I?"

She giggled. "Did you did outdid yourself? Yes, you did outdid yourself."

"I must have, you're wearing part of it."

She looked down just as he reached over and flicked her chin. "You brat!"

"Me? You ran into my finger with your face. How is that my fault?"

They dissolved into laughter.

Summer doubled over and ended up leaning on his shoulder. It was kind of nice, so she didn't bother moving. Or objecting when he put his arm around her.

"Are we watching this or not?" he said with a fake grumble.

"Play it." She reached over and pressed the play button.

Summer spent most of the movie in a pleasantly drowsy daze of fullness, warmth, and comfort, snuggled against Ben.

Being with him like this was such a welcome change of pace from the drama and anxiety and racing around of her normal day to day. All the things that weighed her down didn't seem to have as much power here, curled up on his couch.

All in all, this was not a bad way to spend a day and she didn't want it to end.

Chapter Twenty-Three

Ben's arm fell asleep somewhere around the time Jack Sparrow found the chest reported to hold the heart of Davy Jones. By the time the movie was over, he'd lost all feeling, but there was no way he was going to move with Summer snuggled against him.

He kept expecting her to fall asleep, but every time he looked down, her half-open eyes were still watching the screen.

When the credits rolled, he flipped the television to a documentary on dolphins.

Summer held her thumb up. "Really committed to this ocean theme, aren't you?"

"Yup. When I commit, I really commit."

She shifted her head and looked up at him. "I feel like there was a cryptic message in there."

He widened his eyes. "Cryptic? I thought I was being obvious."

She sat up and tilted her head. "Ben."

He raised an eyebrow and waited. "Yes?"

"What are you doing?"

"Just waiting."

"For what?"

He studied her face. Her hesitation, her wariness of what he might say. Heck, he wasn't entirely sure what he was about to say, but here goes nothing. "For you to admit we should give this a shot."

"Ben. We're friends. Practically siblings. We grew up together."

"Yup."

"We've never had so much as a conversation about anything other than that."

"We're having a conversation now."

"It would be totally weird." She got up and folded the blanket, putting it neatly at the end of the couch. "I should go."

He hadn't wanted to upset her, but she was right about one thing. They'd never talked about this. Or anything like this. But the fact that she knew exactly what he meant told him the thought had at least crossed her mind.

"Do you want me to clean anything up?"

"Everything's already cleaned up, Summer."

"Oh. Okay." She hurried over to the door and slipped her feet into her shoes.

Ben got up and walked over to her. "Let me know what you want to watch next weekend."

Her hand fluttered up and pushed a loose strand of hair behind her ear. "Oh. I'm not sure it's a good…"

He lifted one shoulder and let it drop. "Let me know."

She pulled the door open.

Ben put his arms out for a hug. Summer stepped into his embrace.

He wrapped his arms a little too tight, and his hopes soared when she melted into him and her fingers curled into the fabric of his shirt. He brushed his lips against her hair and felt her shudder.

He pulled back and looked down at her. She met his gaze with wide eyes, her lips ever so slightly parted. He knew without a shadow of a doubt that if he moved an inch, right now, right this second, and kissed her, she would kiss him back.

Instead, he put his lips next to her ear and whispered, "You're right. This is totally weird."

Chapter Twenty-Four

Summer jerked back and planted her fists on her hips. "Ben!"

He laughed and put his hands on the sides of her face and kissed her forehead. "Let me know what we're watching next weekend."

"I said it might not be a good idea." Her heart fluttered and her knees were still weak after that close encounter.

He gave her a cocky grin. "Yeah, I heard you. Let me know by Wednesday at the latest so I have time to plan the menu."

"It just so happens that I have a date next weekend."

"With Johnny Pee Pants? Tell him I said hi."

She drew herself up to her full height and crossed her arms. "Are you calling me a liar?"

"One hundred percent."

"Wow." She grasped at straws. "Maybe I'm going out with Isaac."

"Not a chance."

Summer wanted to get the smirk off his face. "Why? You think he wouldn't date me because he's super rich or something?"

He was completely unbothered by her manufactured

outrage. "*You* wouldn't date *him*, despite him being super rich, because he's a Bingley. Besides, you already shipped him with your sister."

Okay, so he had been paying attention. "I can't believe you just threw this at me out of the blue."

He crossed his arms and leaned against the door frame.

"Okay, fine, maybe not completely out of the blue, but still." He'd thrown her completely off by holding her close like that, then almost kissing her, and then pulling back and making a joke. She'd also thrown herself off by wanting him to kiss her. Where had that come from? It didn't make any sense. This was *Ben*. Ben who'd tricked her into eating dog food once, thrown frogs at her at least a dozen times, pushed her into the creek more times than she could count. (Which would be roughly equal to the times she pushed *him* into the creek, but that's beside the point.)

She shook her head, trying to clear the swirling thoughts. "I'll talk to you later. Sometime. Whenever. Maybe. I'll see you when I see you." She went out the door and down off the porch, satisfied with having the final say.

Ben called after her, "Pick an Italian movie. I'll make my gourmet meatballs."

Exasperated, she jumped into her SUV and left without another word. She wasn't sure what frustrated her more, that he almost kissed her when she wasn't sure she wanted him to, or that he pulled away when she realized she definitely did.

The sky was fading to a gorgeous orange and yellow glow as the sun set. It made the perfect backdrop for the brilliantly colored leaves that were getting close to the peak of autumn splendor.

She wasn't sure about this situation with Ben. Everything was so comfortable and easy with him, but was that only because he was so familiar? Was it because she was in the time frame for a rebound? She rejected that notion as soon as she thought of it. Her relationship with Michael Mastriano had been brief and had never progressed beyond surface level. No emotional entanglement, no rebound.

She also wasn't sure if Ben was interested in her as she was right now, or some outdated idea he had of her from the past.

She slowed and put on her left turn signal. She waited for two oncoming cars to pass before she could turn onto her lane. As she turned, a fresh new sign caught her attention.

A brand new wooden sign with a warm stain hung properly, its fresh gold letters proclaiming, "Welcome to Willow Creek".

When she was fully in the driveway, she jumped out of the car and ran over to inspect the sign.

The wood was entirely fresh, with deeply carved lettering and subtle etched willow fronds framing the edges of the sign. She ran her fingers over the words. The lettering had been colored with a shiny gold paint with reflective specks, and then filled in with a sort of resin. It was brilliant, actually, because the letters wouldn't get gunked up with road dirt from passing vehicles.

She walked around and saw both sides were identical, welcoming guests coming from either direction.

A horn honked. She jerked around and saw Gavin waiting to pull in. She ran over to her SUV and pulled up to the house.

"When did that happen?" she asked when they were both out of their cars.

"Friday. I helped him hang it before our... entertaining guests arrived."

"They were awful, weren't they? Poor Trina. I felt so bad for her."

"Me, too. I saw her one friend was recording the brawl all the way into the creek."

Summer's eyes went wide. "Oooh, wouldn't it be hilarious if it went viral?"

"For you and me, yes. For Trina and her fiancé? Probably not."

"Maybe they should play it at the reception."

Gavin laughed. "On a big screen. That'd be priceless."

"Or give out copies as wedding favors. So much more useful than some of the stuff I've seen."

They climbed the steps to the porch and went inside.

Andi and Mack snuggled under a blanket on the couch. Mack watched the television while Andi read a book. Summer was so relieved to see them back to their normal affectionate selves.

Gavin flopped onto the couch beside their mom, while Summer took the overstuffed recliner and popped the footrest up.

He touched the book to maneuver it so he could read the title. "Is that the newest one?"

"Yup."

"Is it good?" he asked.

Andi huffed an offended sniff. "Of course. All his stuff is good."

Summer asked, "Who?"

"Harlan Coben," her mom and brother answered in unison.

Summer and her dad exchanged a look and a head shake. Mack said, "It came in the mail today. She hasn't said two words since."

"Where are Jill and Nana?"

"Bingo."

"Want me to order a pizza?" Gavin asked.

Summer put a hand on her stomach. "Just get me a salad. I'm stuffed."

Andi peered over the rim of her glasses. "What did you have?"

"Ben made surf and turf and lobster mac and cheese and crab dip and these little cucumbers with crab meat. He did a whole ocean theme since we were watching *Pirates of the Caribbean*."

"Speaking of Ben, what's he charging us for that sign?" Mack asked.

"No idea," Summer said. "I thought he was just fixing the old one. I didn't even see it until just now when I was pulling in."

Mack grudgingly admitted, "It's a great sign."

Gavin added, "He said his friend Rowan over in Hickory Hollow did it."

"Looks expensive," Andi said reluctantly.

"I'm sure Ben wouldn't have gotten something we couldn't afford. He knows our situation." Summer hoped so, anyway.

An hour later, they were polishing off their pizza when Jillian and Nana came through the front door.

Nana scowled and made a beeline for her bedroom off the kitchen.

Mack asked, "What's up with her?" just as Andi said, "You're home early."

"Mildred cleaned her out," Jillian said as she tried not to laugh. "Nana's convinced she was cheating somehow because she never heard the caller say 'N37' and that's what Mildred won on. Nana only realized she had it after the caller closed the game."

"Ooooh, throw down in the parking lot of St. Joseph's."

"It was a whole thing. Nana got into a big argument with

the caller who validated Mildred's ticket. They offered Nana an extra card for free, but she told them they were crooks and threw a whole pile of bingo cards on the floor so they told her to leave."

"They most certainly did *not*," Nana snapped from the doorway. She stormed over to her rocking chair and sat. "I decided it was time to leave. I will not be treated that way."

"Mom," Andi said. "This is the third time you were kicked out of bingo for causing a scene. They're going to ban you."

Nana snorted. "Not if they know what's good for them."

Summer bit her lips to keep from laughing. "On that note, I think I'm heading to bed."

Jillian and Gavin both made their exits as well. As Summer headed up the stairs, she was a little bit envious that they were both leaving to go to their own homes. Living at home was great, and having a little break from paying rent was amazing, but she needed her own space.

Chapter Twenty-Five

After Sunday dinner at Rosie's Diner, Ben snatched the check before his parents could grab it.

"Benjamin." Charlie said sternly, reaching for the check.

"Father." Ben held it out of reach and got his wallet out.

"You need to save your money for the future."

He could record this conversation and play it at random intervals across the span of ten years and it would always go the same way. "I am saving money for the future. I am also spending some money now to treat my parents to lunch."

"Charlie, let him be."

"Now Susie, we can't let him spend all his money on us."

"Dad. It's thirty bucks for a few sandwiches. You guys spent more than that on the groceries I ate at your house last week."

"Yes, but you're doing work for us and not charging like you should."

"I promise, it's all a wash." For a little seasoning, he threw in, "Besides, I use that free work for elderly clients as a charitable contribution for a tax break."

"Charitable! We're not poor. We want to pay you."

Susie put a hand on his arm. "He's teasing you."

Charlie sat back in the booth. "Well, we're not getting dessert next time. And we're just getting water. No sense in you spending three dollars for a soda."

"Speak for yourself. I'll be having my Diet Coke."

"You shouldn't be drinking that."

Susie narrowed her eyes. "I'll thank you not to police my beverages."

"It's true. Those artificial sweeteners are bad for you."

"Shall we discuss the preservatives and artificial ingredients in those snack cakes you have to have every day with your lunch?"

Ben sipped his own soda – regular, not diet – and watched his parents have the same discussion they had every time they were at a restaurant.

"Or the bacon cheeseburger slathered with mayonnaise you just had? Or the chocolate cake with an inch of peanut butter icing? I bet your doctor would be pleased to hear about that."

He grumbled and backed down.

Ben handed the check and his card to the waitress.

Charlie waited until she walked away. "Why are you putting that on a credit card? You'll be paying interest on this meal for years."

"It was my debit card. Same as using a check."

"Oh."

He appreciated that his parents were concerned about his financial security, but sometimes it got on his nerves. Like now.

"Are you and Summer dating now?" his mother asked.

Hold up, maybe the money conversation wasn't so bad. "What? Where'd you get that?"

"Francine said she saw Summer's car parked at your house

yesterday. I assume that's why you didn't call me back until late."

"Francine's nosey."

Charlie huffed a laugh in agreement.

"She was just curious. If you don't want people asking questions, be more discreet. Apparently she was there all day long."

Ben hid a smirk. "I think Francine would have been more interested if she'd been parked there all night."

"Benjamin. Summer's a nice girl."

"She'd still be a nice girl if she spent the night."

Susie's eyes widened. "Has she? Are you two…"

"That's really, really, *really* none of your business. Or Francine's. So let's not have this discussion ever again." He softened the words with a smile. "Unless you want me to ask questions about what you and dad do some nights." He would never, never, ever ask those questions. Not ever. Not even if his life depended on it. Nope.

Her cheeks pinked. "Benjamin Matthew Keller."

"Didn't think so." He laughed and signed the slip the waitress handed him.

He drove his parents home and gave his mom a kiss on the cheek. "I'll talk to you later."

His phone dinged while he was driving home. He ignored it, assuming it was his mom, texting to make sure he made it home okay, and by the time he pulled into his garage, he forgot about it.

He was in the middle of switching his laundry from the washer to the dryer an hour later when his phone dinged again.

Playing hard to get?

Summer's message ended with a smiley face emoji.

He swiped to read her first message.

Do you have a minute?

He decided to go along with playing hard to get. Instead of calling her immediately, which was his first impulse, he texted her back.

Just saw your message. What's up?

I wanted to talk to you about the sign.

He smiled as he replied.

Sign? I'm a Scorpio.

You know what sign. It's beautiful.

Glad you like it.

I thought you were just fixing the old one.

Couldn't be fixed. Rowan said the wood was rotting.

What do we owe you?

Nothing.

What do we owe Rowan?

Nothing.

Ben. That's a hugely expensive sign. I was googling what a custom sign like that would cost and even the low end ones were a fortune. How does it cost nothing?

> Had all the materials already, and Rowan owed me some labor from when I helped build Sarah's she shed.

I'm not sure I believe you.

> I promise. We swap work all the time. I had the wood and stain, and gave him a few bucks for the resin. No big deal.

It's a big deal to me.

He wasn't sure how to respond to that. He was still thinking when her next message came in.

> And obviously he put a rush on it because it was done so fast.

> I can give you his number if you don't believe me.

She called his bluff.

That'd be great.

He typed out Rowan's number and sent it. For the longest time, she didn't respond, so he put his phone in his pocket and started the dryer. The chores never seemed to end. He swept the kitchen floor and started the dishwasher and was back out in the garage gassing up the lawn mower before she sent him another message.

> He confirmed your story, but I don't feel right taking it for nothing.

Ben could understand that. He supposed he might have

overstepped a little bit in ordering the sign. And it wasn't until this very moment that it occurred to him that he should have waited and gotten some input in case they had a different vision for what the sign should look like. Oops.

His finger hovered over the keypad as he debated how to word his apology.

> I'm sending him and Sarah a gift card so they can go out for dinner.

He was thinking of a way to say he loved that idea when she messaged again.

> I'm not buying YOU dinner though.

His fingers flew over the keys.

> I'll buy you dinner. What time should I pick you up?

> Didn't you see enough of me yesterday??

> Nope. I'll be there at five.

> Five? Are we doing the old people early bird special? Six.

> Deal.

> You're ridiculous.

> You're beautiful.

> Wow, you're pulling out all the stops.

> You have no idea.

What's that mean??

Instead of answering, he clicked his phone off and slid it into his pocket. Let her wonder what he meant, when in reality he hadn't meant anything at all. But he'd let her stew.

Chapter Twenty-Six

Summer waited for a response, but none came. "What a brat," she grumbled, then put her phone in her pocket.

"Game's on," her dad called from the living room.

Summer grabbed a drink for each of them and settled on the couch to watch football. She wasn't overly invested in any particular team, but her dad was a diehard Philadelphia Eagles fan. He was decked out in his green jersey and ballcap and loudly belted out the "Fly, Eagles, Fly" anthem even after the television cut away for a commercial.

"We're going all the way this year," he often told anyone who would listen.

During the first commercial break, Summer said, "I was thinking of doing some new ads on social media. We've got three spring weddings booked already, it would be nice to get the calendar filled up."

"How are you coming with the vendor event?"

His question startled her. "I thought you didn't like that idea."

He shrugged one shoulder. "I didn't at first, but it makes sense. Might be better to focus on that and getting everything done in The Shoppes, and then use the income from the vendor thing to pay for ads. We can also use that time to revisit our pricing structure since you said it was outdated."

"Really?" He'd balked when she suggested raising their prices to be more in line with what their competitors were charging.

The game came back on and all conversation was over until the next segment. She mulled over his suggestion and he was right. Instead of booking weddings at their current prices, she could quietly focus on the repairs and upgrades and after the event start advertising and booking weddings at a higher rate.

A wave of guilt flowed over her. Since she'd gotten back, she and her dad had butted heads so much that she dismissed his ideas outright. That had to stop. He'd done a complete one-eighty and stepped back to let her do her job. Now it was her turn to step back and stop thinking she knows better about the business than he did.

The Eagles scored a touchdown.

Her dad mirrored the referee's signal by shoving his arms up in the air. He held his breath until the kicker scored the extra point.

When it cut to commercial again, Summer said, "Vanessa at Spicy Cider is interested in partnering with us for the event."

"Sounds good. The winery events like this always seem to draw a big crowd. Just make sure they're responsible for the carding for the alcohol." He looked skyward, thinking. "Might want to call Ryan and make sure our insurance allows alcohol on the premises for an event like that or if we need a special policy."

"Most weddings serve some kind of alcohol," she pointed out.

"Yeah, but those are private events. This would be open to the public."

"Good point." Definitely a good point, and it humbled her a little that she hadn't considered the distinction. She made a note in her phone to remind her to check with their agent Monday morning.

From there, she settled in and half-watched the game while she scrolled social media on her phone and made more notes as she randomly thought of things to add to her week's to do list.

"Looks like somebody's out front," her dad said midway through the fourth quarter.

"Probably Ben."

"You don't have him working on a Sunday, do you?"

"No, he's taking me to dinner."

"Hmm."

"Don't start."

A minute later, Ben rapped twice on the front door and came in without waiting for a response, like he'd done since he was about eight years old and Andi told him to quit acting like a guest.

He stopped and dripped water on the rug in the entryway. "Might want to grab your raincoat. It's pouring."

She scrunched up her nose. "Yikes. Did you get that wet just coming from the truck?"

"Yep. If you don't mind, I think we'll just go to Slices since it's the closest thing."

"Sounds good to me. Dad, you want me to bring a pizza home for you guys?"

"Sure." He sat forward, focused on the tied game, as if his concentration would zap his team with an extra boost of luck. Without looking away from the screen, he said, "You be careful out there."

Summer put on her boots and jacket. Out on the front porch, she looked at the downpour. "Ugh, this is ridiculous."

"I'll go first and open your door."

Before she could object, he ran down the steps and splashed through puddles on the sidewalk. He opened her door, then ran to the other side of the truck. Rain or not, she took notice that he'd parked with her door closest to her so he'd take the bulk of the rain.

She sprinted for the truck and dove in, but in a downpour this heavy, it wouldn't have mattered if she took ten seconds or ten minutes to cross the yard.

"It looks like it's ten o'clock already."

"Yeah, I didn't think it was supposed to do this."

He'd left the truck running, so it was warm. Summer turned the fan speed up on the heater.

Ben carefully turned the truck around in the parking lot and drove out onto the road. He flipped his lights to high beams.

The rain was so loud on the roof there was no point in having a conversation. The wipers whipped back and forth at top speed.

They'd gone about a mile when she caught something blue in the headlights. "What is that?" As they slowly got closer, she said, "Plastic bin."

"Probably somebody moving and lost it."

The hair on the back of her neck stood. Her chest tingled and something in her gut screamed that something wasn't right. "Ben, pull over. Stop the truck."

"What? Here? There's no—"

"Please!"

He eased over to the shoulder and threw his four-ways on. He hadn't even put the gearshift into park before Summer unfastened her seatbelt, jumped out of the truck, and raced back to the bin. Her heart pounded as she grabbed the lid and popped it up.

Terrified eyes shrank back.

"Oh no, oh no, oh no."

"What is it?" Ben splashed up beside her.

Summer grabbed the bin and almost dropped it because it was much heavier than she expected.

Ben grabbed it from her. "What is it?"

"Kittens." Her voice caught and she nearly choked on the word.

The bin had holes punched in the lid. Holes that allowed the torrential downpour to get inside.

Ben ran back to the truck, splashing through the slop. Summer kept pace with him and wrenched the back door open.

He slid the bin across the back seat. "It's not safe to stay parked here."

Summer climbed into the back seat and put her seatbelt on.

Ben ran back to his seat and eased the truck onto the road.

Summer popped the lid off again and sucked in a shaky breath. A mother cat and four, no, five small kittens huddled in the corner of the bin, shivering on top of a soaking wet blanket and an inch of cold water.

"It's okay, mama, it's okay." She whispered reassurances around the lump in her throat.

The calico cat hissed but made no move.

She brushed helpless tears from her cheeks. "Ben, what do I do? I don't know what to do." She put her hand under the corner of the bin the cats were in so the water would shift to the opposite side.

"Are they okay?" he asked over his shoulder. The wipers thumped rapidly as the rain poured down.

"There's so much water in here and it's so cold."

"Hang on." He put the turn signal on. "We're almost there."

Summer looked away from the cats. Streams of water

flowed down the window. She squinted into the darkness at two pinpoints of light ahead. It took a little bit to recognize they'd turned down the road to Ben's house. He pulled into his garage. The sudden quiet was disconcerting. He jumped out of his seat and wrenched the back door open. "Put the lid on."

She gasped at the suggestion. "Ben, I can't, it's cruel."

He calmly said, "We don't want her to try to escape."

She snapped the lid on but felt like a monster doing it even though he was right. If the mama ran off, the kittens were surely doomed.

He carefully slid the bin out the driver's side while Summer clambered out her side. She opened the door that connected the garage to the house. "Where to?"

"Bathroom. Grab some towels," he said as he carried the bin back the hallway.

She yanked the linen closet open and grabbed an armload of towels.

"Lay them in the bathtub."

She spread the towels in the tub while he ran out of the bathroom and back in a minute later with the quilt from his bed. He got on his knees beside the tub and quickly lined it with the quilt.

"Easy, mama, we're here to help," he said as he took the lid off the bin.

Summer took the lid and put it behind her on the floor. The mother cat hissed again and trembled.

Ben said, "You hold the bin, I'll try getting them out."

The position was awkward, and she was closer to the bathtub. "It's too heavy. You hold it and I'll get them."

He angled the bin so the water pooled away from the cats.

"You first, mama." Summer braced for the cat to bite or scratch, but all she did was give another half-hearted hiss as Summer scooped her out of the bin and into the tub. She hurried to lift the kittens out and put them with their mother, who sniffed and licked each of them while warily keeping an eye on the humans hovering around her.

Ben shoved the bin out of their way and reached back to the cupboard behind the toilet, where he produced a stack of hand towels.

Summer wriggled her coat off and took some towels. Working in silence, they picked the kittens up one by one and dried them off as much as they could.

The mother cat eyed them suspiciously, but lay down on her side.

Four of the kittens immediately nuzzled her belly, looking for milk. The fifth kitten didn't move.

"Ben." Summer's heart seized as she grabbed his arm.

"Here." He gently lifted the still kitten and wrapped it in a towel and handed him (her?) to Summer. "I'll get the heating pad."

Summer sat with her back against the tub, cradling the tiny orange bundle against her chest. "It's okay, baby, it's okay."

Ben rummaged in the linen closet until he found the heating pad. He plugged it in and turned it to the lowest setting. "The cord won't reach that far."

He helped Summer get to her feet. She sat on the toilet seat and wrapped the heating pad around the towel bundle in her arms.

Ben said, "You're freezing."

"Doesn't matter." She hadn't even noticed until he mentioned it.

"Let me get your shoes and socks off."

Never taking her eyes off the sweet bundle in her arms, Summer lifted one foot, then the other, as he tugged her boots and soaking wet socks off. He disappeared again, then came back a moment later with a pair of thick woolen socks. He bent down and pulled them onto her feet. "That should help a little."

"Thanks." She couldn't tear her eyes away from the little orange cat in her arms. "He's awake at least."

His little green eyes were barely open, but he was looking around a bit.

"Are you okay if I run to Tractor Supply? I'll get some cat food and see if there's any kitten milk or anything."

"Please be careful."

"I will. I'll be back as soon as I can."

She heard his footsteps as he literally ran from the bathroom back through the house to the garage.

It took a while, but the kitten stopped shivering. She feared the worst, but his eyes still moved. The mother cat was busy grooming her babies in the bathtub. She stiffened every time Summer moved.

"Who did this to you?" Summer's voice broke and whatever protective dam around her feelings broke and she burst into tears. How could someone be so cruel?

Chapter Twenty-Seven

The rain had slowed significantly by the time Ben wheeled the shopping cart to the truck. He hurried to shove the items in the back seat and splashed back through the puddles to return the cart.

He had to remind himself to take his time and drive slowly. The entire drive home was full of what ifs. If Summer hadn't demanded that he pull over... It felt like forever before he pulled into the garage. He grabbed the most important things first, hauling in a bag of cat food, a litter pan and bag of cat litter.

When he reached the hallway, he heard Summer sobbing and assumed the worst, that the poor orange kitten hadn't lasted for the hour it had taken him to get supplies. He steeled himself and stepped into the bathroom.

Summer cradled the kitten, wrapped in a towel and heating pad, but little orange ears perked toward the sound of Ben's arrival and its eyes tracked his movement.

The mother cat was busy licking her kittens, who had created an adorable, if still wet, pile of kittens in the corner of the tub. He counted and all four of them were moving. His shoulders relaxed a fraction. At least she wasn't upset over the worst case scenario he'd feared.

"Hey."

She sniffled and looked up. Her chin quivered as her eyes filled with more tears.

"Is he okay?" He asked about the cat, but he was more concerned about her. Her big heart was surely breaking for these poor animals.

She unspooled a handful of toilet paper to blow her nose. With a shaking voice, she said, "I don't understand how someone could…" She waved the toilet paper toward the tub.

"I don't know." He really didn't. What kind of monster could abandon them in such a horrible way?

She took a deep breath. "I called the police but they said there's not much they can do."

He leaned down and kissed the top of her head. "You're amazing, and you saved their lives."

"Yeah, but if—"

"No. Don't do that. There are a million things that *could* have happened, but the only thing that matters is what *did* happen." He ran a hand over her damp hair.

The orange kitten let out a pitiful mew and the mama cat stood up and put her paws on the edge of the tub, looking for her baby.

"Hang on, mama, I'll give him to you." Summer handed him the heating pad and carefully unwrapped the kitten from the towel. He squirmed as she put him in the tub near the others. The mother cat immediately sniffed him all over and nudged him toward the pile of his siblings.

Ben was relieved the cats all seemed to be okay, and that was all they could focus on for now. He set up the litterbox beside the tub and picked up the bag of cat food. "Oh. Guess I need a bowl."

That earned him a small smile.

"I'll be right back." He got two bowls he didn't use very often and filled one with water and one with food.

Summer said, "I don't think they like the food to be with the litter. Maybe put the food by the sink?"

He didn't know much about cats, but that sounded logical. He moved the dishes.

"What are we going to do with them?" she asked.

"I don't know. For tonight, I think they're good here in the bathroom."

He watched her look around the room.

"Can we put this stuff in a drawer or something?" she motioned to his shaving things. "If they get up here somehow, they could get hurt."

"Yeah, of course." He gathered the items and put them in the linen closet, then double checked that the door fully latched. He scanned the room for anything else that might be sharp or dangerous, but came up empty. "Let me give you some clothes. You're freezing."

Summer hugged herself and shivered.

They looked in on the cats again. The orange kitten was finally nursing, while most of the others were fast asleep. He looked at each one until he saw their little sides move as they breathed. Mama cat's eyes were half-closed, but her ears shifted with every sound.

Poor thing was probably exhausted.

He moved to let Summer pass him, and turned on the little nightlight he used when his niece and nephew stayed over. Her hair was still wet, so he grabbed the hair dryer and took it with him as the left the bathroom.

"Here," he said as he motioned to his bedroom. "I'll get you some clothes and you can dry your hair."

"Thanks." She gave him a tired smile.

He gave her a pair of sweatpants, one of his favorite hoodies, and another pair of thick socks, then grabbed dry clothes for himself and left her to change. He changed clothes in his tiny laundry room, knocking his knee painfully against the dryer as he maneuvered in the small space.

He flopped onto the couch and turned the television on while the hair dryer whirred from the bedroom.

A few minutes later, Summer joined him in the living room. She shifted the curtain to look out the window. "It looks like the rain finally slowed down, thank goodness."

"It was better when I was heading back from Tractor Supply." He watched her for a moment. "Do you want me to take you home?"

She looked back the hall. "Are you going to keep checking on them? And keep me posted? Please?"

"Of course." It caught him a little off guard to realize the amount of trust she had just shown.

She sucked air through her teeth. "Oh, crud. I forgot I told Dad we'd bring pizza."

"We can still bring pizza. I'll call it in and we can pick it up on the way." He called in the order while she went back the hall to check on the cats.

Monday morning was a slog. He'd gotten out of bed to check the cats every two hours or so, and he was feeling the lack of sleep.

Diane looked up as he dragged himself into his shop. "You look terrible."

"Thanks," he said with a smile.

"What's the matter?"

He yawned. "Nothing. Just up a million times last night checking on a family of stray cats we picked up."

She perked up. "Stray cats? Where?"

He gave her the whole story. "Right now they're safe and relatively comfortable in my bathroom."

"My sister used to foster cats, but stopped when she had to help take care of her in-laws. I know she's been itching to get some cats. Do you want me to call her?" She already had her phone in her hand.

"Yeah, you can give her a call, but I need to check with Summer to see what she wants to do."

Chapter Twenty-Eight

Summer stifled a yawn. True to his word, Ben had texted her every few hours through the night, sending her pictures of the cats safe and sound. As soon as she was in the office, she googled to see if she could guesstimate how old the kittens were, and from her search, she figured they were about four or five weeks old.

Her kitten research stalled when she got an unfamiliar notification on her phone. It took a few minutes to realize it was the new automated scheduling Isaac had helped her set up on their website.

Andi was in the storage room, organizing the linens from Willow Hall so they could inventory what they had, what needed repaired, and what needed replaced.

Summer yelled over, "Hey, Mom! Guess what!"

She appeared in the doorway with a half-folded tablecloth. "What?"

"We just got a bride who scheduled a consultation to look at the facility. I just confirmed, so she'll be here tomorrow."

"Nice. I stand corrected. I thought adding that to the website was going to be a waste."

Summer's mind immediately went into to do list mode. "Did we finish the bathrooms in Willow Hall?"

"Everything's done in there, but those spindles still need fixed on the gazebo. I'll get your dad to take care of that today."

"Perfect. I'll put the info packet together and see if Jillian got her new flyers in yet."

Andi said, "She did. I think they came last week. I'll go grab a handful."

"Thanks." Summer turned her attention back to the computer so she could print out a blank contract and information sheets they gave to every potential client. Once that was done, she let the folder open on her desk so she'd remember to add Jillian's flyer, then grabbed her clipboard and went to do a quick walkthrough of both event buildings.

She was pleased to see everything was ready to go in Creekside Hall. The garage door company had come and fixed all the rolling doors so all eight of them went up *and* down like they were supposed to.

The storage room was mostly organized. All the Creekside Hall linens had been laundered, and the stained or damaged ones had been put off to the side to be dealt with later.

The fire extinguisher inspection turned up another faulty extinguisher, so Mack insisted on all of them being replaced. All three buildings had new extinguishers located in several discreet but easily accessible places. The fire escape maps had been updated and posted as required.

Most of what was left was cosmetic work in Willow Hall, and the repairs to the gazebo.

She went to the gazebo and looked off at the creek that had swelled from the previous day's rain. The water was muddy and fast-flowing.

"I'm really proud of you," her dad said from behind her.

Summer spun around. "I didn't hear you coming."

"That's 'cause I'm a ninja." He sliced the air with his free hand. "Super stealth. My enemies never see it coming."

She laughed. "How many enemies do you have?"

He wiggled his eyebrows. "None, anymore."

"Thanks, Dad. I know the past month hasn't been easy for anyone."

He shrugged one shoulder. "Change never is. But you've done a great job, and I'm more than a little frustrated with myself. We got all that stuff done in what, six weeks? Stuff that I've been putting off for a year or more. I should have been on top of all this. And I shouldn't have dug my heels in like I did. It's pretty embarrassing to think I acted worse than a two-year-old."

"Dad, stop. It's easy to get behind, especially when you have to deal with Nana's health issues on top of your own. Mom's Super Woman and she got behind, too. I'm just glad I could help and we're getting back on track." She didn't address the rest of it. She'd let it go, and he could work through it however it suited him to.

He slung an arm over her shoulders. "I think your sister should put a sunflower field in over there." He pointed to a spot across the creek.

"I think that's a great idea."

"Probably be able to make some money with local photographers when they're in bloom."

"You should mention it to her." She wasn't sure if Jillian would be interested in that or not.

"I think I might. But first, I need to get some measurements for this railing. It's probably not going to be painted in time for your meeting tomorrow, but I'll have the spindles fixed."

She gave him a squeeze.

"Oh, and I sent you a link."

She touched her back pocket. "I must have left my phone in the office. What is it?"

"Nice apartment for rent out there on Baker Street. Furnished. I know you've been wanting your own space."

"You're trying to rid of me," she teased.

"You can stay forever as far as I'm concerned, but I think it's probably better for you to separate work and home. That's not easy to do when you live at your job."

"You and Mom do it."

"Yeah, and it's not always easy." He cleared his throat. "I can go look at it with you, if you want. Make sure it's good."

"Thanks, Dad." She didn't mention that she'd come across the listing herself. Nope, he could take all the credit and be hero dad.

Chapter Twenty-Nine

Ben had never been so glad to see the end of the work day. This had been the Mondayest Monday that ever Mondayed. The coffeemaker in the office quit working, and when he ran to Walmart to get a new one, his company card was declined because it had expired at the end of September, which Diane had reminded him about at least four times. He had a client file a dispute and get a chargeback on their credit card for work they'd completed back in June, and he'd bit his cheek – hard – when he tried to eat his lunch.

On the upside, Diane's sister was more than happy to take the cats. He needed to talk to Summer first, but he was glad to have a plan for them.

He got home and checked on the cats. The food was gone, and the litterbox had gotten a workout. He scooped the clumps into a plastic bag and refilled the food and water bowls.

Then he ate a quick supper before giving Summer a call.

As soon as she answered, she said, "Hey, how are the cats?"

"Good. I left the bathroom door open, and mama cat

ventured out into the hallway a bit, but then she went back to the kids."

"Nice. How was your day?"

He blew out a hard breath and flopped onto the couch. "A long, long comedy of errors. But a comedy like Shakespeare where everybody gets poisoned and no one laughs."

"I think that would be a tragedy."

"Today was a tragedy, so that tracks."

"Can I come see the kittens?"

"Of course, Summer. You don't have to ask." That would be perfect, then he could talk to her in person.

She was there in twenty minutes and as soon as he let her in, she made a beeline past him toward the bathroom.

"What am I, chopped liver?"

She ignored him completely. "Hi, babies, how is everybody?" she asked in a singsong voice.

Ben leaned in the doorway, just watching her shower love on the cats. The mother cat leaned into her hand and purred. The orange kitten perked up and watched her every move.

"This breaks my heart. They had to be living in someone's home. Someone's pets. And then just thrown away like that." She looked up at him. "What are we going to do?"

"I think we have a really good solution. Diane and I were talking about it this morning."

"Sorry if I should already know this, but who's Diane?"

"My office manager. Her sister used to foster cats, but she stopped taking them in when her husband needed help caring for his parents. So she called her sister and she's willing to foster the cats and find them homes. Diane says it'll probably end up being a foster fail and she'll keep them all."

"All of them?" Summer scratched the orange cat's head.

"I mean, nothing says we can't find homes for one or two of them ourselves."

"Aren't they too little to be away from their mother?"

He assumed so, but had zero cat experience. "Diane said her sister would know all of that."

"What do we know about this sister?"

He tried not to crack a smile at her suspicion. "I've met her a few times, and I've known Diane forever. She's been a friend of my mom's for years. I'm sure your mom knows her, too."

"I'll see if she knows the sister. What's her name?" She pulled her phone out.

"Deb. I'm not quite sure what her last name is."

She gaped up at him, incredulous. "How am I supposed to look her up on social media if we don't have her last name?"

"I don't think we need to internet stalk her."

"I'm not stalking. I just want to make sure she didn't go to prison for stealing cats or something."

In the end, he convinced her to start with calling her mom, who, yes, knows both Diane and Deb, and yes, they're both lovely women who have never been to prison, so Summer decided to put the FBI-level sleuthing on hold.

"I wanted to check with you before I called her. In case you had a different plan."

She scratched the orange kitten's head. "Unfortunately, I don't. As much as I'd like to, I don't think I can reasonably take six cats."

"Me, either." He didn't mention that he'd considered keeping a kitten. Or two. Particularly the little orange furball nuzzling Summer's hand. Just in case it didn't pan out, he didn't want to get her hopes up.

Summer made a resigned face. "I suppose you can call her. It's probably our best option. Mom said she'd love to have cats, but Nana's allergic so we can't have them in the house. I'm *not* taking them to the pound."

"Absolutely not. They've been through enough."

She looked up at him. "What made today so bad?"

He lifted one shoulder and let it drop. "Just one of those days. It's much better now, though." He winked and made her laugh. "How about you? How was your day?"

"Great. I have a consultation tomorrow with a bride who used our new online booking system."

"Sweet. Is that the one Isaac recommended?"

"Yes. I have to tell you, he's had some great ideas that I hadn't considered. Guess I don't know everything after all."

He mimed zipping his lips shut. "I'll never tell."

"No, you'll just keep it in mind and rub it in whenever you can."

"Every chance I get, forever and ever."

"Brat."

Chapter Thirty

Tuesday was bright and sunny. The creek had receded, and the lawn was freshly mowed. Summer double and triple checked every detail. The only thing out of place were the unpainted spindles on the gazebo. She hoped that tiny thing wouldn't bother the bride.

At nine fifty, a black SUV slowly turned onto the drive.

Summer dashed out of the office and down the stairs with the packet in hand, along with a clipboard and pen. Her stomach rolled with nerves. She wanted so badly to make a good impression and start filling the bookings calendar.

She greeted the four visitors with a bright smile. "You must be Alicia." She reached out to shake her hand.

"I am. And this is my fiancé, Jack, and my parents, Tina and Ed."

"Nice to meet you all." Summer exchanged handshakes. "Did you have a nice drive in?"

"We did. The leaves are stunning."

"They are, aren't they? October is my favorite time of year." She got down to business. "Let me show you around. How many guests are you planning for?"

Jack answered, "Around a hundred and fifty."

"Great. Let's start in the new facility. We call it Creekside Hall." She led them across the stone pathway that connected the buildings, giving them a brief history of the property. Her nerves calmed as she slipped into this familiar role.

In Creekside Hall, she'd set up one table, fully decorated, to give them an idea of how the space could be utilized. "Typically the DJ sets up over here," she pointed, "and we have the dance area here."

"Very nice," Tina said, snapping pictures of the space.

"Depending on the weather, we can raise all or some of these doors." She pressed a button for the closest rolling door. Once it was up, she said, "If it's nice, a lot of people move out here to dance and mingle."

"Is there an extra charge to use that space?" Ed asked.

"Not at all. Since there's no roof, we wouldn't feel right charging more in case you aren't able to use the space due to the weather. Any other questions for this area?"

"I don't think so," said Alicia.

"Perfect. We'll go out this way and I'll show you the gazebo."

They walked along the stone pathway to the gazebo.

"We had to replace some of the spindles. Of course they'll be painted to match the rest."

Alicia nudged Ed. "Looks like your back porch."

He groaned a little. "We had some branches come down and take out part of our railing. It's fixed but of course with the rain we couldn't paint."

"It's an epidemic," Summer joked.

Alicia asked, "Will we be able to take pictures here?"

"Of course, as long as the weather is cooperating."

"Is there an extra charge for that?" Ed asked.

"Nope." Summer led them to Willow Hall. "This space has a

bit more rustic aesthetic, so whether you want Creekside Hall or Willow Hall will really depend on the vision you have for your wedding. Both have approximately the same capacity for guests."

Ed looked around. "What are the odds of having two weddings on the same day?"

"We only book one major event for any given date."

"If we book the date now, can we decide on which building later?" Tina asked.

"I'd ask that the building selection be made within a few weeks. While we won't book another wedding for that day, there could be a shower or birthday party or some such event in the other space."

Alicia nodded. "I'm still filling my Pinterest board."

"I totally get that. We also have a florist and a baker on site if you haven't chosen those already."

"Would that cost extra?" Ed asked.

"Yes. You would contract for those services separately. I have flyers included in your packet."

Tina said, "This is a lovely venue. We toured one other place this morning. Can we call you after we've had a chance to discuss the options and let you know?"

"Of course."

"Can we look at the first building again?" Alicia asked.

"Absolutely." Summer led them back across the path into Creekside Hall.

"Sorry, I don't want to be a pain."

Summer pushed the door open and ushered them inside. "You're definitely not being a pain. We want your special day to be exactly what you want. If you've thought of any more questions, I'm happy to answer."

"Are we required to use your baker and florist?"

"Not at all. And they're independent businesses, so even if

you don't use this venue, you can certainly order your cake or flowers through them."

"Okay, let's get the bottom line," Ed said with a sigh.

"Sure. Let's have a seat."

They all sat at the table and Summer opened the packet and pulled the blank contract out. She pulled out another sheet and said, "Here's the pricing." She pointed down the page with her pen. "And here is everything that includes."

"What if the headcount changes?"

"That won't affect your pricing at all for the space. It would really only apply for your caterer or perhaps your wedding planner. Here's the maximum number of guests, which would include the bridal party."

"But if we need more tables, that's not an extra fee?"

"No, this covers all the tables and chairs you'll need. We can also provide black or white tablecloths for no additional charge. If you want linens that match a specific color scheme, you'd need to provide those. Once you have a more solid number, we can discuss round or rectangle tables and how you want those arranged. We have enough of both to set up in whatever configuration matches your vision for the day."

"What if we have a band instead of a DJ?" Jack asked.

"No problem. They'd be set up over here, just like a DJ. We have plenty of outlets for their equipment."

"Where would the caterer set up?"

She pointed over her shoulder with her pen. "This room behind me has lots of counterspace and an island for caterers who will be serving food so they have room to prep. If you're doing a buffet-style meal rather than table service, we typically set up the buffet tables this way. If you're having a bartender, that would be here." She motioned to another spot.

Alicia looked at her dad and nodded as a grin spread

across her face. "I don't think we need to talk about it. It's perfect."

He reached into his jacket pocket and produced a check-book. "Okay, let's get this part over with."

Summer went over the contract with him, making sure Alicia was following along, and filled in the blanks as they talked. He initialed each paragraph as they went. Before he signed it, he said, "Can we add a note that we have three weeks to decide which building we want?"

"Certainly." Summer looked at the calendar in her phone. "That would be October 27. I'll just make it the end of the month to make it simpler." She wrote a line at the bottom of the contract, which he initialed. Then he signed and wrote a check for the deposit.

Summer slipped the check under the clasp of her clipboard and rose. "We'll head over to The Shoppes and I'll make a quick copy of this before you go. There are displays in the lobby, so you'll be able to see samples of the cakes and flower arrangements."

A few minutes later, she left them to flip through the albums both her siblings wisely kept on the counter in front of their respective businesses. She jogged up the stairs and copied the contract, then hustled back down.

Alicia was oohing and aahing over the four-tier cake Gavin had in his display case while Tina showed Ed pictures from Jillian's album. "Oh, this is lovely."

Summer smiled as the door opened and her sister walked in. "This is Jillian. She's the owner of Jilly's Blooms and she did all of the wonderful arrangements you're seeing. Jillian, Alicia and Jack are getting married here in June. These are her parents, Tina and Ed."

"Congratulations. If you have any questions about flowers, I'm happy to help."

Alicia said, "Do you have any suggestions for what flowers to use?"

Jillian nodded. "I always recommend peonies first. They're one of my personal favorites, and they symbolize happiness and romance, which is perfect for a wedding. They come in a variety of colors." She flipped through a few pages of her binder and settled on a photo of a lush bouquet. "These are peonies."

"They're so pretty."

Summer stood back and let her sister take the lead on the flower discussion, which ended with her giving Ed her business card.

He tapped it against his palm. "We'll be in touch."

"Thank you so much," Summer said.

"Thank you," Jillian echoed.

Summer walked over and held the door for them.

"I'll email you about the building," Alicia told her.

"No problem." She gave them a little wave as they walked to the SUV.

"That went really well," she said to Jillian.

"Yeah, they seem nice. Thanks for talking up my arrangements."

"Why wouldn't I? You do incredible things with flowers, Jill. You're very talented."

Jillian seemed surprised. "Thanks." She shifted uncomfortably. "Um, while you're here, can you maybe come into the shop for a minute?"

"Sure." She followed her sister past rows of plants, to her desk in the back.

"I was going over the books. Here's what Mom and I originally agreed on for rent, but I honestly don't know how you could expect me to catch up on all the back rent that Mom didn't collect."

"I don't."

For the second time in as many minutes, Jillian looked surprised. "I mean, you came at me pretty hard about not paying it."

"To be fair, I was trying to defend myself. Is that original amount feasible going forward?"

"What, you'll just say I don't owe it and then hold it over my head later?"

Summer wished she knew why her sister had such a low opinion of her. "No, I'll talk to Mom. If she wants to forgive anything that's outstanding, and I assume she will, then we just start fresh on November first. If she wants you to pay any back rent, that's between you and her."

"What about Gavin?"

"I have no idea what agreement he came to with Mom, but he did pay rent for this month, based on his original agreement."

"How could you not know what agreement they came to?" Clearly, Jillian didn't believe her.

Summer bit her tongue before she answered. She made sure to temper her tone and not snap at her sister. "Because it's not my concern. I'm so focused on how we move forward that I don't have the bandwidth to worry about what went on previously. I worked seventy-five hours last week. Trust me, I do not have time to care about your back rent or Gavin's."

Jillian hesitated. "But he paid rent for October?"

"He did."

Before she could say anything more, Summer said, "I'm meeting Isaac for lunch. We're going to go over optimizing our social media advertising, so maybe you want to come along. He's had some great ideas that I'm sure could be helpful for you, too."

"Oh."

"I guarantee he won't mind. You might as well pick his brain while he's in town."

"Maybe..."

Summer decided to try extending an olive branch. "Grab your laptop and come along. We're leaving in like ten minutes." Maybe if they could get on civil footing, she might be able to find out exactly why Jillian couldn't stand her.

Chapter Thirty-One

Wednesday evening, Ben opened the front door to let Deb in. Summer sat on the living room floor with her back against the couch. The orange kitten was fast asleep on her lap, while two others snoozed against her leg, and the other two tentatively explored the space under the coffee table. The mother cat was curled up on the couch, after Ben told her a least a dozen times she wasn't allowed on the furniture.

"Oh, look at these babies," Deb cooed. She got down on the floor near Summer and picked up one of the kittens from under the coffee table. "I'd say you were spot on. I'd estimate them to be five, maybe six weeks old."

"What will happen to them?" Summer asked.

"I'll be fostering them in my home. We have a vet appointment for Friday, when they'll likely get their first round of shots and get scheduled for spay/neuter. Then we'll start looking for forever homes."

Ben watched Summer protectively stroke the orange kitten. "Are they old enough to be away from their mother?"

"Not yet," Deb assured her. "The youngest we even consider separating kittens from their mamas is eight weeks, but twelve is ideal. I personally don't allow adoption until ten weeks. We want to make sure they have the healthiest, best possible start."

Ben said, "What kind of screening process happens?"

"All of the adoptions take place through the agency. They conduct criminal background checks, check with the potential adopter's current veterinarian, that sort of thing. You can look on the website and you'll see all the information on the application page." She picked up each kitten, one by one and inspected their undersides. "We've got three girls and two boys. They'll all be fixed before they're adopted, too, as will their mama."

"The police said there's not much they can do about the people who dumped them and left them to die. Is there anything *we* can do?" Summer asked.

Deb's smile dropped and turned to a dark scowl. "We can't do what I'd *like* to do to people like that." She stroked the pure white kitten with one black ear, who was investigating her shoestring. "Unfortunately, there's nothing we can do, either, unless we find out who did it. And it makes me sick because we hardly ever find out who does these things. At least this bunch has a happy ending to their story."

A few minutes passed as they all focused on the kittens.

Deb spoke again. "I'll be completely honest. At least a couple of them will be adopted by me and my husband. We had to stop fostering when his parents were ill, and we've both really missed having cats."

"Definitely keep us posted," Ben said. "It'd make us both feel better to know they're all in good homes."

"Of course." Deb stood and unzipped her carrier.

Summer whispered into the orange kitten's ear, "Goodbye, Storm."

Ben pretended not to hear.

The mother cat was none too pleased when they started putting her babies in Deb's cat carrier. She was livid when she went to investigate and Deb scooped her in the carrier with them. She swiped a furious paw at Deb, who yanked her hand back in time and seemed unfazed by the attempt.

When they were secure, Deb carried the yowling cats to the door. Ben put a hand on Summer's arm before she could stop Deb and he was suddenly the official owner of six cats.

After Deb left, Summer stood, staring at the door, her mouth downturned at the corners. Ben pulled her close for a hug. "You okay?"

"It feels silly to be so attached after two days."

"It's not silly at all." He had a few pangs himself about letting them go.

"I can't even *have* a cat right now." She looked up at him with wide eyes filling with tears. "You think they're in good hands?"

"I think they're in great hands."

"Should we make a donation to the rescue to help cover the costs?"

"I gave Deb a check."

"You did? When?"

"Right when she left." He lightly tapped the tip of her nose. "You might have been a little distracted."

"Just a little."

"Summer." He waited until she looked up at him again. "They're in good hands, and they'll all have wonderful homes."

She let out a long breath. "I know." She rested her head on his shoulder and squeezed his middle while he rubbed her back.

"Tell me about your meeting with Isaac." He figured it might be good to shift her thoughts away from the kittens.

She let go of him and went over to sit on the couch. "It was great. We had some social media ads running, but they were set up a long time ago and of course the algorithm has changed since then. Probably more than once. And really significantly. He showed me different targeting options and how to optimize the budget and stuff like that. It's crazy how fast this stuff changes. It's an entirely different system than when I studied it in college."

"You're not kidding. Diane took some kind of online class for ads back in the spring. She said it was really helpful. I can get the info from her if you want." He was glad he had Diane handling that side of things. It was outside his wheelhouse.

"Sure." She leaned toward him with a sparkle in her eye. "Guess what."

"What?"

"Jillian went along and Isaac was giving her some tips as well. He could not keep his eyes off her."

"Nice."

She chuckled a little. "I'm not sure she noticed, though."

"You don't think she likes him?"

"I think she does, but I don't think she thinks he likes her. Or maybe she's just ignoring it because he'll be leaving soon."

Ben stretched his arm out along the back of the couch and touched her shoulder. "I thought he was only going to be here a week?"

"He said 'a few weeks' so I'd imagine he'll leave soon. Sending him my way was a great idea. He's been very helpful."

Ben flicked a stray piece of her hair. "I have lot of great ideas."

"Oh yeah? Like what?"

"Like you and me." He wiggled his eyebrows and grinned, but this time she didn't smile back.

"What if I don't want to stay in Willow Creek?"

Chapter Thirty-Two

The words surprised both of them. It had been a nagging thought in the far recesses of her mind, but it's not like she had been contemplating leaving. Or contemplating staying, for that matter. Everything was happening so fast and seemed to be so dramatic that she hadn't taken the time to consider what she really wanted for her own future.

"Is that… Do you want to leave? Go back to Chicago?" Ben asked carefully.

"Maybe? No? I don't know. It's not like I'm planning to leave anytime soon, but we both know I didn't exactly come back home because I *wanted* to come back home. If I hadn't been forced out, I'd still be there."

"Do you wish you were still there?"

She didn't have to think about the answer. "No. I'm glad I'm home, but I don't know what the future looks like."

"Nobody does."

She gave him a side-eye. "That's awfully deep."

"I'm just saying. Aren't you looking at that apartment tomorrow?"

"No, she left me a message and said she needs to reschedule."

"But you are planning to get a place and presumably sign a lease?"

"Yeah."

"Which would suggest you're planning to be here for at least a year."

"Sure. But what if we get involved and then in a year I want to move?"

"Then we move."

"Just like that." She was skeptical. Ben's whole life was here. His friends, his family, his business.

He answered as if she'd said the words out loud. "Your whole life is here, too, Summer. You didn't lose your family or your friends or anything when you went to Chicago. Just because I haven't moved away doesn't mean I couldn't, or wouldn't, go to Chicago with you."

"I do know that I don't want to go back to Chicago. But I've thought about going somewhere else. Maybe Atlanta or Dallas or Boston or Juneau. I don't know."

"How about Honolulu?"

She couldn't tell if he was serious. "I'm not sure I'd want to live off the mainland, just in case I have to get home for an emergency."

"Juneau isn't considered mainland."

"You know what I mean."

"How about Miami? Jenna lives there."

Summer sighed again. He was being far too reasonable about this.

"Okay, so is that part of your five-year plan? And don't even tell me you didn't update your five-year plan since you got back."

Yes, she had a five-year plan. No, she hadn't updated it. "I figured I'd be here at least two years. I need to get the business back to where it needs to be, and then we need to implement systems to ensure it continues running smoothly."

"There you go."

"What about your five-year plan? Or ten? I'm sure it includes a picket fence and a bunch of little Bens running around the yard with a golden retriever or two." She sat back, just out of reach of his fingertips.

"It doesn't."

"No?"

"Okay, maybe the golden retriever. But I never saw my life with kids. I have Taylor and Kyler and I'm the best uncle ever. Like, *ever*."

"No doubt."

"I knew when I was a teenager that I wouldn't have my own kids."

"How did you know?"

He scooted closer and leaned forward to look her straight in the eyes. "Because even then I knew I wanted to spend my life with you, and having kids of our own wasn't going to happen."

Her heart pounded, the blood drumming in her ears. She jumped up and crossed her arms. "That's not fair. It's not my fault you decided to not have kids."

He gave his head a shake. "No, don't try twisting what I said."

"You said you didn't want kids because I can't have them."

"Close, but no cigar. From the time I was about fifteen, every time I pictured my future, you were in it. I never envisioned kids in that picture. Sure, kids are great, but my life is full without them. I don't feel like I'm missing anything, and I never did. And after your surgery, that just sealed the deal." He ran a hand down over his face. "This is all coming out wrong. I'm not saying you're responsible in any way for me not wanting kids. I just want you. I always have, no matter what that looks like."

Summer turned in a slow circle, not sure what to say. When she faced him again, she said, "That's a lot."

"I know."

"I don't know how to respond. I'm overwhelmed and tired. I want to go to bed and put a pillow over my head and not come out for a month. I can't look you in the eye and say I'm ready to jump into a committed romantic relationship right now. I know I love spending time with you and when I'm with you, I feel calm and safe and more like myself than I do anywhere else. But I don't want to lead you on or whatever I've been doing and then end up hurting you. I'd never want to do that."

"I know. I didn't mean to upset you. I'm just laying all my cards on the table."

"I'm not upset. I'm just overwhelmed, and I know I'm being completely wishy-washy, and I'm sorry about that. Every decision I've made lately has been the wrong one, and the last thing I want to do is make the wrong move with you. You're too important to me."

Ben gave her that sly half-smile of his. "That's a start. Go home and get some rest. Clear your head and come to the obvious conclusion that I'm perfect."

"Too far, Ben."

He chuckled and planted a kiss on her forehead. "Drive safely, Summer."

She drove home, carefully paying attention to her speed and her surroundings. Which worked out perfectly, because she had to slam on her brakes to avoid colliding with a deer that bounded across the road in front of her.

Pulling up to the garage, she noticed the lights were still on in The Shoppes. She walked to the main doors, intending to turn the lights off, when she heard clanging and the thump of music.

"Gavin?" She called.

"In here," he answered from the bakery.

She went inside, pulling the scent of fresh-baked cake deep into her lungs. "This smells amazing. What is it?"

"Pistachio."

"As in, the little green nuts?" She went around the counter to the baking area where Gavin was surrounded by mixing bowls and spatulas and cakes pulled fresh from the oven.

"One and the same."

"Huh."

"It's delicious." He grabbed a fork from one of the stainless steel drawers and dug into the smallest round layer of green cake. "Here, try."

"Did you just give me a bite of a client's cake?"

He jerked his head toward her, incredulous. "Of course not. I always bake an extra layer for a test. Try it."

She took the fork and blew on the cake to cool it before she ate it. "This is amazing. What kind of frosting goes on this?"

"This one is getting a rosewater buttercream."

"Sounds fancy."

He eyed her. "What's on your mind?"

She sighed heavily. "Ben. Storm. Everything."

"What storm?"

"The kitten. Storm. I know I wasn't supposed to name him or get attached, but here we are."

"Did that lady come get them tonight? Is that why you're bummed?"

"Yes. Partly." She filled him in on her conversation with Ben. "It just seems like a lot that he's willing to not have kids because I can't, and he's so ready for a relationship and I don't know if I am."

"Hold up," Gavin said. He let his spatula rest in the bowl of frosting he was mixing. "I don't want to make you feel worse, but it's not like Ben just sat here for years pining and waiting for you to come home. If he wanted kids, he had plenty of opportunities to get married and have them. You're not that special." He punctuated his last words with a snort-laugh.

"Jerk."

"Diva."

That made her grin. "Snot face."

"Bubble head."

"Toe jam."

"Hunchback."

Now they were both laughing. She fired, "Troll."

"Goblin."

"Dragon breath."

"Chicken fart."

She was laughing so hard she could hardly manage, "Lizard poop."

Gavin bent over the counter, holding his stomach as he guffawed. "Worm fart."

Summer jumped off her stool and pointed at him. "You lose! You lose! You already said fart!"

"Dang it."

She wiped the tears from her eyes, but couldn't quite stop laughing as she settled back on the stool.

When she left the bakery an hour later, she was full of cake and feeling better. She could always count on Gavin to be a straight shooter and tell her what she needed to hear, even if she might not like it.

Chapter Thirty-Three

Ben spent the evening second guessing himself. He knew he'd come on a bit strong, laying down exactly what he thought. He hadn't meant to make her feel like she was responsible for any of his life choices. If he knew Summer at all, he figured she'd go quiet, taking a day or two to process their conversation.

In the meantime, he gave her space, but on Thursday, he still went grocery shopping for the ingredients for his meatballs. Best case scenario, she'd come over on Saturday and they'd watch a movie and eat too much. Worst case scenario, he'd have an entire batch of meatballs to himself. Which was still a pretty darn good deal. His meatballs were top notch.

After stashing his groceries at home, he headed back to the office, where Diane gave him his marching orders to visit three job sites.

At the first, he calmed down a very young homeowner who was insisting they stop painting her walls white because she'd picked out blue paint. Ben had to explain three times that the white paint was primer and not the final color. Then he had to calm down his painter, who was about one more silly complaint away from walking off the job.

The second stop was far less pleasant. An elderly couple in the midst of a kitchen remodel complained that one of his workers asked them to cancel the job so he could come back and do the work cheaper for cash under the table. He pulled his foreman aside.

"What's going on? Where is he?"

Mike shook his head angrily. "I fired him on the spot. I know that's not following procedure, and I apologize for that, but when I called him on it, he got up in my face."

"How are the Andersons? Anything I should know before I go talk to them?"

"Nah, they're fine. Confused, mostly."

Ben went in to speak with the Andersons.

"I hope we didn't get that young man in trouble," Mrs. Anderson fretted after describing how he'd suggested his "deal" not once but twice.

"We had to let him go. That was completely unacceptable."

"I hate to see him out of work." She looked at her husband. "Maybe we could give him some small jobs?"

"Absolutely not," Mr. Anderson said firmly. "Anyone working in this house better be licensed and insured."

"I sincerely apologize for this whole thing. I want to assure you we don't tolerate dishonesty in this company. As you mentioned, we're fully licensed, insured, bonded, and we guarantee our work. We value the trust you've placed in us by allowing us into your home."

"I appreciate you coming out," Mr. Anderson said, struggling to his feet and holding out a hand.

Ben stood and shook his hand. "And I appreciate you talking to Mike about this so we could address it. Our integrity is the most valuable thing to me."

"As it should be."

He stopped and filled Mike in on their conversation. "Go

ahead and offer Mrs. Anderson that higher end faucet set she originally wanted for no extra charge. It won't affect the bottom line much, and hopefully that smooths Mr. Anderson's feathers."

"You got it, boss."

The third stop was a piece of cake. One of their new plumbers just wanted someone to double check some seals he'd installed before he closed the ticket.

It was dusk by the time Ben headed for home. He rounded a bend and collided with a brick wall. At least, that's what hitting the deer head on felt like. The airbag punched him in the face while the seatbelt locked, jerking his chest painfully, forcing the air from his lungs. His limbs flailed, out of control. His right knee hit the underside of the dash and his left arm bashed against the window.

He gasped for air and immediately coughed violently, sending crushing pain through his chest so intense he thought he might lose consciousness. Or maybe he did. He wasn't entirely sure. The powder from the airbag coated the inside of his nose and stung his eyes. It smelled like smoke and blood.

He lifted his shirt to cover his nose and mouth and slowly took stock of his situation. Steam rose from the crumpled hood of his truck and he turned the ignition off.

His ears rang, he wasn't sure if it was from the airbag deploying or the actual crash.

He struggled to pull in much of a breath and guessed one or more of his ribs might be cracked. No head injury that he could ascertain. Arms and legs accounted for, although pain started to filter in through the shock. He unclicked his seatbelt and reached to the passenger seat for his phone. It wasn't there.

He waved his hand in front of his face, trying to clear the

smoke, until he realized it must be the airbag powder in his eyes making everything fuzzy.

He pulled the door handle but nothing happened except a pain in his hand so intense he was afraid he'd vomit. He reached across with his other hand to grip the handle and shoved his shoulder against the door. It wrenched outward about two inches and stopped.

The climb over to the passenger side was brutal. Every inch he shuffled sent excruciating pain throughout his chest, but he managed to scoot over and push the passenger door open.

Footsteps pounded toward him. An unfamiliar voice called, "Are you okay?"

He turned and the teenage boy took a step back.

"Dude, you are not okay."

The powder made its way to his throat and he started a coughing fit that was fire in his chest. He was bent over coughing when he saw his cellphone on the floorboard. He grabbed it, but the thing was as useless as a brick. It must have hit the dash. The screen was covered with a fresh spiderweb of cracks, and the power button did nothing.

"I called 9-1-1," the kid said.

"Thanks," Ben rasped.

"Should you like sit down or something?"

It was probably a good idea, but there was nowhere to sit along the side of the road.

"You could like sit in like my car if you need to."

"Thanks," he rasped again and gingerly made his way across the shoulder of the road to where the boy's Honda sat idling with its four-ways blinking. Another coughing fit overtook him. He gripped the guide rail and leaned over it as his stomach threatened to empty. He put a hand up to cover his mouth as he coughed. When he pulled his hand away, there was blood. "I'll just lean here. Don't want to get blood in your car."

The boy hesitated. "Okay."

"I'm Ben."

"Cooper. My mom's on her way. We live just over there." He pointed vaguely down the road.

Ben nodded. Breathing hurt too much to talk. He tried to assess any other injuries. There was definitely something going on with his hand. It was difficult to see, but his face felt fine. He supposed there was some level of shock, because the way the kid looked at him, he knew his face was definitely not fine.

Cooper's mom arrived less than a minute later. She parked her SUV on the shoulder behind Cooper's car and put her four-ways on before jumping out of her car.

"Are you okay?"

Ben almost answered before he realized she was talking to Cooper.

She walked around the car to Ben. "Are you alright?"

He nodded again. "I'm fine. The deer came out of nowhere."

"Let me call 9-1-1."

"I already did," Cooper told her. "I didn't know what else to do."

Ben tried to smile but he didn't think his mouth moved much. "You're doing great, Cooper," he wheezed.

Sirens screamed in the distance. Seconds later, the bright lights cut the darkness as the emergency vehicles rounded the corner. Two police cars arrived on the scene, followed almost immediately by an ambulance.

One officer talked to Ben, while another inspected the front of his truck and the deer.

An EMT came over to check him over. "That's a lot of blood. You should go to the hospital."

Ben nodded and stood to walk toward the ambulance, but a sharp pain in his chest and sudden dizziness doubled him over.

"Whoa, hang on there, buddy."

He motioned to a second EMT, who pushed a gurney across the asphalt.

Ben wanted to object, that they didn't need to make a fuss, but another wave of dizziness prevented him from saying anything.

They loaded him on the gurney and into the back of the ambulance. As they put an oxygen mask on him, he caught a glimpse of Cooper's worried face and managed to give him two thumbs up.

The back door slammed shut and a moment later the ambulance jerked away and sped toward the hospital.

Ben relaxed back onto the gurney, letting the EMT take his vitals and answering his questions as best he could through the airbag powder in his throat and the oxygen mask covering his mouth.

At the hospital, lights from the ceiling blinded him as he was wheeled down a long hallway, through a set of wide automatic doors, and into a small curtained room where a team of nurses assessed the situation.

"Is there anyone you want us to call?"

His memory was fuzzy, and he hadn't memorized a phone number for nearly a decade. His first thought was to call his mom, but his brain couldn't recall her number. He rattled off the only one he could remember completely.

Gavin's.

Chapter Thirty-Four

Summer left the bank frustrated. She'd tried to deposit the check Ed had given her, but the teller had grimaced and told her there had been a stop payment put on it.

When she stopped to pick up pizza and salads to take home for supper, they hadn't started her order.

Annoyed, she sat at a table and scrolled through her phone for half an hour until they called her order number.

She picked up the pizza box and peeked into the bag of salads. "I ordered four salads."

The woman at the counter rolled her eyes and called back to the kitchen. "I need another chef salad!"

Summer bit her tongue. They weren't even that busy.

Finally, the cook dinged a bell and put a salad on the pass through window. In a bowl.

The woman rolled her eyes again and yelled, "That's to go!"

The salad disappeared from the window and a minute later, a to go box was tossed onto the pass.

"Here ya go."

"Thanks," Summer muttered. She set the salad container – which wasn't in a bag and had no dressing – on top of the pizza box with the bagged salads. She awkwardly carried her food order out and set it on the back seat.

On her way through town, both lights turned red just as she pulled up to them. By the time she hit the lane that would take her home, it was mostly dark, which ramped up her annoyance. She hated the days getting shorter, especially since the temperature dropped exponentially after the sun went down and she hadn't taken a jacket when she left the house because it had been warm out.

Without taking her eyes off the road, she reached over and turned the knob on the heater. Warm air blasted on her legs.

She slowed down for the upcoming S-turns. As she rounded the second turn, she saw two pickup trucks off the side of the road and a still-burning flare. She slowed to a crawl. One of the trucks sported a completely smashed front end. The second truck, parked in front of it, had the tailgate down. Two men were hefting a dead deer from the road onto the back of their truck.

As she drove past, both men jumped into the cab of their truck.

She passed them and they sped out behind her, their tires spinning stones from the shoulder. They tailgated her through the S-turn, then sped out into the wrong lane and passed her, still in the oncoming lane as they entered the next set of blind curves.

"Idiots!" she yelled even though they couldn't hear her.

It wasn't until she pulled into her driveway that the smashed truck suddenly seemed too familiar.

It looked an awful lot like Ben's.

She parked haphazardly and grabbed the food from the back seat. Her shoes slapped against the pavement as she ran into the house. "Where's Gavin?"

Her parents looked up from their spots on the couch.

"I don't know."

"Beats me," her dad said.

They seemed completely normal, so maybe she was overreacting. Half the guys in this town had trucks, and half of those looked a lot like Ben's.

"I have food." She carried it to the kitchen. Once she set it down, she pulled her phone out of her back pocket and called Ben. Her call went to voicemail. She sent him a text, then called Gavin. Again, no answer.

She tried calling and texting over and over as she managed to eat a slice of pizza and a few bites of salad.

"What's going on?" Andi asked.

"There was a wrecked truck on my way home and it looked like Ben's. He's not answering his phone."

As the last word came out, her phone rang. Gavin.

"Hey, what's up? I was in the shower so I missed your call."

"Have you heard from Ben?"

"No, why?"

She told him what she'd told her parents.

"Huh. No, I haven't heard from him. I was going out to get some groceries, so I'll swing by his place and see if he's home. I'll call you back."

"Thanks, Gav."

They hung up and she felt better. If anything had happened, Gavin would surely know. She fought the urge to call Ben's parents. There was no use in worrying them for nothing. She ate her salad.

Fifteen minutes later, Gavin came through the door, calm but urgent. "I had a voicemail. Ben's at the hospital. Let's go."

Summer's heart jumped in her chest. "Gavin?" Her voice was an octave too high. She was suddenly freezing cold.

"Is he okay?" Andi asked.

"She said he's awake and alert and he'll be fine, but he's pretty banged up. I saw the truck on the way here. He's lucky."

"Don't be speeding to get there," Mack warned.

"I won't."

Summer snatched her jacket from the hook. "I'll call you," she told her parents.

Gavin led the way, running across the yard and jumping into his car. Summer got in the passenger seat and buckled up as Gavin fastened his seatbelt and pulled out of the driveway.

"Did they say anything else?"

"No, just what was on the voicemail."

"I feel horrible. I didn't even talk to him today or text him. The last thing I said was that I need space and now he's in the hospital. What if it's worse than they said? What if he's not okay?"

"I don't think they can tell you someone's okay if they're not."

She sat rigid in her seat for the entire twenty minute drive to the hospital, scanning the darkness for deer. Thoughts whirled through her mind. She was worried about him, but was it because he was like a brother to her, or was it something more? Why couldn't she give him a straight answer?

"Because you're afraid to."

"Huh?"

"You just said, 'Why couldn't I give him a straight answer?' That's why. Because you're afraid."

"What if I'm not afraid, I'm just not sure?"

Gavin pulled into a parking space and turned in his seat to face her. "Summer, if you weren't sure, you would have flat out told him no. You're being all wishy-washy because you know what you want, you're just afraid of it for a whole lot of reasons. Some of which are valid."

His words had the ring of truth, but right now, they had more pressing matters.

He nodded once, then got out of the car. Together, they hurried across the parking lot. Gavin spoke to the nurse at the front desk while Summer paced and chewed on her thumbnail. A few long minutes later, another nurse came through the wide doors and led them back through a maze to the heart of the emergency room.

For a second, Summer wasn't sure they'd been led to the right person. Ben's face was bruised and his eyes were swollen nearly shut. Dried blood caked around his nose and cheek. A bandage was taped onto his forehead. A tuft of bloodied hair stuck out from it.

The half of his mouth that wasn't swollen turned up at the sight of them. "Hey, guys," he rasped.

Summer pushed past Gavin. They crowded onto the one side of his cot that wasn't full of flashing, beeping machines.

She reached down and took his hand. "Ben? Are you okay?"

He croaked, "Can you call my parents? My phone was destroyed and I can't remember their new numbers."

"No problem." Gavin was on it immediately.

"What happened?"

He coughed once, grabbing his chest as he did, then answered, "Bar fight. You should see the other guy."

"I'm glad to see your smartassery is still intact. And I saw the other guy being loaded into the back of a pickup truck." If he was joking, that was a good sign, right?

"It was a big one. Lots of meat, I'm sure."

"After what it did to your truck, I can't imagine all the good meat isn't squashed." Summer shuddered.

Gavin said, "Eh, even if that whole side was crushed, that

leaves the other half, probably a good three hundred pounds of good meat for free."

Ben added, "Yup."

"Enough about the freaking deer meat." She couldn't believe this was the conversation they were having when Ben was obviously in bad shape. "Do they know the extent of your injuries? That bandage is pretty big, and there's a lot of blood. Did you hit your head? Do you have a concussion? You keep touching your chest. Is there something wrong with your heart?"

"They couldn't find it."

"What?" Okay, she knew this hospital didn't have the most stellar reputation, but what kind of cracker jack operation couldn't find a heart? Almost as quickly as she'd gotten outraged, she realized he was teasing her.

"Told them I didn't have one. Gave it to you."

"Ben. I'm worried sick and you're cracking jokes." She wasn't sure if she wanted to throttle him or cry. Maybe both. Probably both.

"Sorry. I have a cracked rib and a broken finger."

Summer gasped and looked down at the hand she clutched with both of hers. It looked fine.

He continued, "Mild concussion is likely. The worst part was the eye flush that lasted forever and the tetanus shot because I couldn't remember when I had my last one."

"How long are they keeping you?"

He squinted up at a clock on the wall. "I think they said until 2 AM."

"What? They're not even keeping you overnight? That's outrageous. I'm going to talk to someone."

He squeezed her fingers. "No, you're not. All I want to do is go home and change clothes and go to sleep."

"I thought you weren't supposed to sleep after a concussion? What kind of place is this?" Her voice rose.

"Shhh," Gavin warned. He tried calling Ben's parents again.

Ben assured her, "That's what I asked. Staying awake after a mild concussion isn't necessary. They do want someone with me for the next twenty-four hours, but that's it. I'm allowed to sleep. Which is what I need. It's impossible to get any rest in here."

"Then what?" She felt bad making him talk, but hearing his voice reassured her that he was going to be okay. Even if his voice was gravelly and slow.

"I have to call tomorrow and schedule a follow-up with my regular doctor. She'll probably want to put a split on this." He held up his left hand, where his middle and ring fingers were bound together with a few strips of white tape. His fingernails were caked with blood.

"Did they give you anything for the swelling? Especially your eyes? That looks so painful."

"Just the eye flush. I had an ice pack on for a bit, but it lost its cold."

"Do you need another one?"

He shook his head against the tiny flat pillow. "I need to go home and get some sleep."

Gavin said, "Susie, hi, sorry to call you so late. Ben's fine, but his truck had a little incident with a deer. His phone was destroyed, so he asked me to call you. Here, I'll let you talk to him."

Summer let go of Ben's hand so he could take the phone.

"I'm okay, just got checked out at the ER. ... No, Gavin's going to take me home. ... Yeah. ... Pretty soon. ... No, you don't need to come. ... Sore, mostly, so I'm sure I'll be laid up for a day or two. ... I will, I promise. ... I know. ... Okay. ... Yup, love you too. I'll call you, oh. I guess I won't call you until

I get a new phone. ... Of course you can come over tomorrow. ... Yeah, you have Gavin's number. Do you have Summer's number? ... Okay, good. ... Love you, too." He handed the phone back. "Sorry, couldn't see the button to end the call."

Gavin tapped on the screen and slid the phone into his pocket.

Ben let his head drop back onto the pillow. "Man, I hope I get out of here soon."

Summer swallowed back tears of relief. He was banged up but ultimately okay. Which meant she had a chance for a do-over of their last conversation and put an end to keeping him hanging.

Chapter Thirty-Five

It felt like forever until they got back home in the wee hours. He lost count of how many times he thanked Gavin and Summer for coming to get him. He'd managed to undress and now stood in a nice hot shower. The last of the dried blood washed off and disappeared down the drain. He could barely stand to wash his face. Every square inch of it screamed in pain when he touched it.

He turned around and braced his hand against the wall, letting the hot water sluice down his back and soothe his muscles. He was not looking forward to the hurt he was in for over the next few days.

He awkwardly dried off and dressed in loose sweats, then padded to the bedroom to sit on the edge of the bed.

"You good?" Gavin asked from the doorway.

"Yeah, thanks, I—"

"Ugh, *please* do not thank me again. I'm pretty groggy, so I'm going to crash on the couch for a couple hours."

Ben nodded.

Summer came in, carrying a glass of ice water and a bottle of over the counter ibuprofen.

He dutifully took the pills and sat still while she put fresh gauze over the butterfly bandages on his forehead, and managed to not whimper when she retaped his fingers together.

"Do you want ice for your face?"

"Nah."

Gavin said, "Dude. You want ice."

"Don't go to any trouble."

Summer left and came back a few minutes later with a plastic zipper bag full of ice from the freezer, wrapped in a thin kitchen towel. "Lay down," she ordered.

He moved gingerly, lifting his legs under the cover. It felt like they weighed a thousand pounds apiece.

Summer fussed with his blanket and then waited while he put the ice pack over his eyes.

Okay, they were right. The cold immediately felt better.

He felt the bed sink slightly as Summer sat down. "You okay? Do you need anything?"

"Nah, just some rest."

"I can go."

He reached out until his fingertips brushed her leg. She wrapped her fingers around his. "You can stay if you want to."

She lifted his hand and shifted around until he felt her curl up beside him. She laced her fingers with his and their entwined hands rested between them. "You know, this was a pretty dramatic way to make a point."

"Man's gotta do what a man's gotta do, right?" He tried to smile but winced as the bruise on his lip protested.

"Don't ever scare me like this again, Ben. That deer really Apollo Creeded your face."

He squeezed her fingers and appreciated that she was trying to joke around a little bit. "Yeah, but did I get the girl?"

There was a long pause. Ben waited but couldn't fight his body's exhaustion.

He hovered somewhere between sleep and awake when she said, "I think you've had the girl for a while."

Voices pulled Ben out of his sleep around eight thirty. He must have slept like a rock, because the bag of ice was still perfectly balanced on his face, albeit melted. He pulled it off and groaned as he struggled to sit up.

Every muscle in his body protested, except the ones in his bladder, which urged him to hurry up. He did his business, then took a long time brushing his teeth to get rid of the lingering taste of hospital and blood and powder out of his mouth.

While he painstakingly got dressed in his bedroom, he heard Summer say from the living room, "No, I understand. I'm sorry you feel that way because I have no idea what you're referring to."

A second later, she said, "He hung up on me. What the heck?"

Gavin answered, "You can sort it out later. Jillian's bringing your car and I'll take her back to the shop."

"Thanks, Gav."

"I think I heard water. Sleeping Beauty might be up."

Ben walked toward the living room with all the speed and grace of a hundred-year-old man.

"Hey, how are you feeling?" Summer came to his side and put a steadying hand on his back.

"Like a million bucks. Might go jogging later." He eased down into the recliner.

"Funny." Summer handed him her phone. "Call your doctor to schedule that follow up."

"Yes, ma'am."

She walked into the kitchen while he called and scheduled the appointment. She came back with a glass of ice water and two worthless ibuprofen.

"They can get me in at three forty-five."

"Great." She studied his face. "Your eyes look less swollen."

"How can you tell?" he joked. He'd seen his face in the bathroom mirror and it was not a pretty sight. The deer had definitely Apollo Creeded him. Two black eyes, a red and purple bruised nose, airbag rash on his cheek and chin and forehead, and a fat lip. But hey, at least his eyes looked slightly less swollen. Progress, he supposed.

"Are you hungry?"

"A little."

"Eggs and toast?"

"Perfect, thank you."

She went to the kitchen. Gavin said, "Jillian's bringing my old phone. We can see if your SIM card still works. It's not great, but it should work until you get a replacement."

"That'd be awesome, thanks." He didn't feel up to spending an hour or two at the cell phone store, which was a lousy task even on a good day.

Summer came in and handed him a plate of eggs and toast. "You should drink more water. Stay hydrated. It'll help you heal faster."

Gavin got to his feet. "Jilly's here."

He went to let her in.

"Hey, Be—wow, you look terrible. They let you leave the hospital like that?"

"Gee, thanks."

"No, I mean... that looks serious." She handed Gavin his old phone.

"It looks a lot worse than it is. Just a cracked rib and broken finger. It could have been a whole lot worse." He kept telling himself that when it hurt to even breathe.

"I'm glad you're okay. Relatively speaking." She handed Summer the keys to her SUV. "I had to move the seat. Sorry."

Summer gave her a tired smile. "I know. The curse of being short."

"Let's get going, I have to finish a cake." Gavin put a hand on Ben's shoulder and squeezed. "If you need anything at all, let me know." He looked at Summer. "You, too. It'll all work out."

As soon as they left, Summer ran to the bathroom. Ben could hear her crying. He hoped it didn't have anything to do with his situation. Maybe it was just because she was tired and stressed? He drained his glass of water. The least he could do for her was stay hydrated like she'd insisted.

He debated knocking on the bathroom door, but didn't want to invade her space and distract her if she needed a few minutes alone.

He heard water running and a minute later, the door opening.

Summer came out and smiled. "How are you feeling? What can I get you? Did you finish your breakfast?"

It was all too bright and forced.

"What's going on?" The conversation he'd overheard earlier came to mind. "Did something happen with that phone call this morning?"

Her face fell and she sat heavily on the couch. She looked completely and utterly defeated.

"Sum? What happened?" He struggled to his feet and went

to sit beside her. "It's not just this, is it?" he asked, gesturing to himself.

She swiped on her phone as tears slipped down her cheeks. "No."

He put his arm around her back, careful not to bump his broken finger.

"It's this." Finally, she tilted her phone to show him the screen. The rating for the farm had tanked overnight to a one star. She touched the screen to scroll through the reviews.

"Owner stole money from me."

"Facility is falling down."

"There are roaches in the bathroom."

"Canceled my wedding with no notice."

"Kicked us out for no reason."

"Rats everywhere."

"Ruined my wedding."

"Racist homophobes."

"Took our deposit and ghosted."

Summer choked back a sob. "It just goes on and on and on."

"These are ridiculous. Nobody's going to believe this."

"Well, somebody does because we just lost Alicia's wedding. I tried to deposit the dad's check yesterday and they put a stop payment on it. I finally got ahold of him this morning and he said they couldn't have their wedding with us because of these reviews. They're afraid we'd cancel or ruin the wedding."

Ben pulled her close. He winced at the pain in his chest, but it was bearable. Seeing Summer cry over these hateful lies was not.

A knock on the door startled them both.

Summer wiped her face and got up to answer the door.

Susie gasped at the sight of her and immediately said, "Is Ben okay?"

He waved from the couch. "I'm fine, Mom."

"Oh, honey, what's wrong?" She gathered Summer into a warm mom-hug and stroked her hair.

Ben answered for her. "Somebody's trolling the farm with fake reviews and they had a wedding cancel because of it."

"That's horrible. Why do people do such terrible things?"

Charlie patted Summer's back and closed the door. He walked over and sat in the recliner and studied Ben's face. "Yep, that's a heck of a pair of shiners you have."

"I'm just glad my nose isn't broken."

"Or your skull. I swear, those deer are like hitting a brick wall if you get them head on. We clipped one oh, two, maybe three years ago, and lucky all we ended up with was a busted headlight and cracked grill. And my split eardrum from your mother screaming, but that's a whole other thing." He grinned.

Ben smiled even though it hurt his lip.

Summer came over and gave him a careful hug. "Since you're in good hands I'm going home and try to explain this to my parents." Her shoulders dropped.

"It's going to be okay." He couldn't think of anything more comforting to say.

"I'll be back in a few hours for your doctor's appointment."

Susie waved a hand. "Don't worry about it, sweetheart. We'll take him. You just take care of this."

Summer sighed. "I wish I knew how." She planted a kiss on the only unbruised part of his cheek and left.

Susie sat beside him and squeezed his hand. "I wish there was something we could do."

Charlie said, "I bet George can do something."

Ben perked up. Jenna's husband was an attorney. Surely he could send someone a letter and get them to back off.

Charlie was already dialing the phone. He put the call on speaker and explained the situation pretty succinctly.

His brother-in-law's voice switched from friendly to professional. "Can you send me some links to these reviews?"

"Yup."

"Where'd you say she was living?"

"Chicago," Ben answered. "Can you send a cease and desist or something?"

"Hmm. You know what? I'll do you one better. I've got some friends in Chicago that work in criminal law. Probably be scarier coming from them than a real estate attorney in Florida. Might cost a couple hundred bucks to find out where it's coming from and see if a strongly worded letter doesn't fix it."

Ben said, "I don't care what it costs."

George chuckled and his professional tone switched back to friendly. "You got it, knight in shining armor."

"He's trying," Susie joked.

"Hey, give Jenna a call. She's worried and it'd do her good to hear your voice."

"I will," Ben promised.

They signed off, and he felt optimistic. He also felt exhausted, which his mother picked up on immediately.

"You go lay down. You need lots of rest to heal. I'll make some soup for lunch when you get up."

He knew he was hurting when he didn't even argue.

He shuffled to his bed and drifted to sleep with visions of Summer, happy and carefree. He wanted more than anything to make that happen.

Chapter Thirty-Six

Summer bawled her eyes out trying to explain the situation to her parents. "It's all my fault. I shouldn't have come home and brought all this drama with me."

Andi rubbed her back, but Mack was the one to comfort her.

"Bullshit!" He exploded. "It's not your fault some piece of trash is pulling this crap."

"I don't know why they'd do this. They already ran Summer out of Chicago, what more do they want?"

It clicked. Nina had to be behind this. There was no other explanation that made any sense. Her despair and sadness quickly transformed to white-hot anger. She wiped her face on her sleeve. "I'm going to go make some calls. Don't worry. Everything's under control."

She jogged to the office and locked herself in. Her hand shook with rage as she tapped on her phone. The call connected immediately. Kayla hissed, "I'll call you right back," and hung up.

Summer frowned at her phone. She was still staring at it

when the incoming call flashed on the screen two minutes later.

"Hello? What's going on?"

Kayla's voice was low. "It's a complete shitshow here right now. Somebody bombed us with a million lousy reviews and Reesa's going absolutely bananapants."

"That's why I was calling you. Someone did the same with me. I thought you might have some insight."

"I don't have much time. I'm hiding in the bathroom. My guess is it's something to do with Nina. Michael Mastriano promised her a PR position on his new show, but they nixed his contract a few days ago, so she went to Reesa and Reesa basically told her to pound sand." Kayla gasped and whispered, "I gotta go."

The line went dead.

That made a lot of sense as to why Nina would go after Reesa. But why her?

And what could she do about it?

She sat back in her chair and stared at the wall, trying to think. It was hard to focus. First and foremost, she was worried about Ben and grateful his injuries weren't worse. Her leg bounced with anxious energy. Maybe a walk would help.

She slipped her phone into her back pocket. As she headed down the stairs, she heard Jillian yelling, but couldn't make out the words.

In the lobby, Jillian and Gavin stood at the counter facing each other. His hands were up like he was helpless against her tirade.

"What's going on?"

Jillian spun and jabbed a finger in her direction. "You. *You're* what's going on. You brought all your poison back with you from Chicago, and now it's infecting all of us. We're the ones who have to pay for whatever you've done."

That was the last straw. Every intense emotion she'd been feeling, all the anger, all the fear, all the worry, all of it burst out. She slapped her palms down onto the counter once, twice, three times, and screamed, "I haven't done anything!" so loud her throat was immediately raw. Her hands burned from the sting.

Jillian stepped back, stunned. Her mouth hung open and her eyes were huge.

Gavin pushed past Jillian and reached for Summer.

She wrenched away from him and ran. She slammed the door open and ran toward the parking lot. A wise little voice told her she was in no shape to drive, so she veered around the far side of Willow Hall and ran for the creek. Her feet pounded across the rickety little bridge. On the other side, she ran as fast as she could, away from the creek, away from the farm, away from everything.

She made a hard right and ran into the corn field. Empty stalks slapped at her as she ran through the rows. The drying leaves bit at her exposed skin, leaving little cuts. She pushed through blindly, running until her chest was on fire and her legs threatened to give out.

She slowed and hit the clearing her internal compass had been aiming for. In the middle of the vast fields was a pond they used to sneak away to when they were kids. Surrounded by corn stalks reaching six, seven, even eight feet tall, she finally felt like she was far enough away.

A large, flat stone had served as a jumping board for generations of youngsters. She climbed onto it and stared down into the water. Her lungs sucked a huge shuddering breath and she cried out in utter frustration and helplessness. Fat drops fell from her eyes and rippled across the calm surface of the pond.

She sobbed until there was nothing left, and the sun had slid from one side of the sky to the other, dipping below the corn. Jillian was right. She'd brought this with her. Instead of swooping in and fixing the farm, she'd condemned it. It was going to fail. Her parents were going to lose their retirement.

Her brother and sister were going to have to find different locations, change their business names. Heck, change their own names to erase their association with her.

Her parents and Nana would have to sell the farm and go live in a tiny shack. She pounded her fists against the rock. It hurt, but the pain gave her something different to focus on.

The sun had warmed the rock, but it quickly cooled, as did the air around her. She hugged her arms around herself and shivered.

As for her? Her career was over. She was doomed to a dead end job in fast food.

A bullfrog's head popped above the water on the opposite side of the pond. His throat puffed out with a loud croak.

A hysterical laugh bubbled to the surface. She yelled at the frog, "DO YOU WANT FRIES WITH THAT?"

He plopped back under the water.

"Summer?"

She gasped and turned.

Gavin walked toward her cautiously. "You okay?"

Her eyes stung, but there were no tears left. "I'm not okay, Gav."

He rushed over and she lifted her arms up for a hug.

Instead, he scooped her up and carried her like he had when they were kids and she'd fallen off her bike and skinned up her knees.

He pushed through the cornstalks.

"I'm sorry."

Gavin snorted. "You should be sorry about all the extra helpings of Mom's cooking. You're breaking my back, butterball."

She cry-laughed against his shoulder. "Maybe you should quit skipping the gym, stringbean."

It felt like the sky darkened with every step.

"I can walk."

He stopped and set her on her feet, but kept hold of her hand.

After a few minutes of pushing through the corn, she said, "I assume she got you and Jillian, too."

"Yup."

"I'm sorry."

"It's not your fault, Summer. Not much you can do up against crazy."

"I think it's Nina."

"Hardwick? The trash tabloid woman?"

"Yeah."

He huffed out an angry sigh. "Like I said. Can't do much against crazy."

They crunched through dried fallen husks and leaves until they came to the edge of the crops.

"Just a tip," he said.

"What?"

"When you're working the drive-thru, maybe don't scream at your customers about fries."

Summer laughed even as her face heated with embarrassment. "Heard that, did you?"

"The entire county heard that."

Her humor quickly faded. "I don't know what to do, Gav."

He stopped walking and faced her. He leaned down a little and gripped her shoulders. "We're going to handle it. All of us. Together. We're a family. A team, Summer. You're not in this alone, and you don't have to fix it by yourself."

"But it's my fault this is all happening."

"No. It's Nina Hardwick's fault, and she's going to stop."

"She won't stop. She's like the Terminator. Only more evil and heartless and vindictive." Her mouth pulled downward. "I left it all six hundred miles behind me without putting up a fight, Gavin, why won't she stop?"

He sighed and slung an arm across her shoulders.

"Jillian hates me even more now."

"Jillian freaked out. She'll be fine."

Summer didn't argue. Even if her sister didn't bring it up again, she'd never forgive her for this. And at this point, Summer wasn't sure she cared. There was probably nothing she could do to have a reasonable relationship with her sister, and with everything else, that was at the very bottom of her list of priorities.

They walked back to The Shoppes. Gavin ushered her inside and steered her toward Jillian's shop.

Summer stopped and planted her feet. "I can't deal with her right now."

"Trust me."

Reluctantly, she followed him past the rows of flowers, back to Jillian's desk. She was surprised to see Isaac.

He stood and reached out to pat her arm. "Jillian was filling me in. I put a call in to our technical team so we can trace where this is coming from."

"I can save you some time. I know it's Nina Hardwick."

His brows pinched inward. "The journalist?"

"If that's what you want to call her."

He flicked his eyebrows up in a knowing way. "Fair. But what does she have to do with this?"

Summer took a deep breath, then explained.

"You're sure it's her?"

"I have no proof, but there's no one else who hates me that much." She shot a look at Jillian.

"I'll send them the info and if you're right, it shouldn't take long to confirm." He smiled a little. "Chin up, we see this every day and we'll get through it."

"What do we do now?"

"Right now? Nothing. We'll work on getting these reviews flagged as fraudulent and hopefully taken down without much fuss or needing to involve the legal team. It'll take a few days, maybe a week, and we'll touch base."

"A week?" Summer hated how pitiful her voice sounded, but she wasn't sure she could take a whole week of this, and she had a sinking suspicion that he was being optimistic.

He put his hand on her arm. "I know it's counterintuitive, but do not engage with this. No responses, no rebuttals, no accusations of fake reviews. Nothing. I'd go so far as to say stay off the internet until we get a handle on this."

"Hurry up and wait," she grumbled. Surely she was an expert at that by now. She just couldn't believe she was enduring this again so soon.

"Sorry. But yes. I'll check in with you in a few days."

"Thank you, Isaac."

"All part of the job."

She caught the glance he cast toward Jillian. This was not part of the job at all.

Chapter Thirty-Seven

Ben sighed and struggled off the couch to answer the unexpected knock on the door just after seven o'clock. His annoyance vanished when Summer walked in with two large pizzas. "I thought your parents would still be here, so I got two."

"Mom was fussing and driving me bananas, so Dad took her home about an hour ago so I could get some rest."

Her face fell. "Do you want me to go?"

"Absolutely not. Bring that pizza over here and sit with me."

She sat beside him on the couch.

Ben turned an old movie on while they ate pizza right out of the box.

"Are you okay?" He asked after she'd been quiet far too long.

Summer laughed a little but there wasn't much humor in it. "Living the dream."

"Did something else happen since this morning?" He reached over and pulled the fuzzy blanket off the back of the couch and put it over their laps. It hurt, but he lifted his arm to put it around her. Once she settled against him, the ache wasn't so bad.

"Lots."

He listened as she told him about the reviews he already knew about – slander if you asked him, or was it libel? – and then about Jillian's accusation. He guessed Jillian had lashed out at Summer out of her own fear and frustration at the situation, but it wasn't much of an excuse. Summer couldn't, and shouldn't, be held responsible for what unhinged person did.

"I'm convinced it was Nina Hardwick. I talked to Kayla very briefly and she said Reesa's going ballistic because they got the same slate of horrible reviews, so Nina's the only person that makes sense."

He agreed that all signs pointed to Nina. "But why come after you? Sure, go after Reesa. She reneged on a job. But you didn't do anything to her."

Summer sighed and flopped back on the couch. "Maybe she thinks I started it all by not marrying Michael Mastriano. If I had gone through with it, he would have gotten his contract with the Family Network and she would have gotten the PR position he promised her."

"I asked George to look into it."

"Jenna's husband? Why?"

"He's a lawyer. I figured he'd have some input."

"I forgot what he did. That was sweet. Thanks."

He didn't mention the part about George's attorney friend in Chicago. No sense getting her hopes up in case nothing came of it.

She snuggled closer and he flinched. She immediately jerked back. "I'm sorry. Did I hurt you? Is it your ribs?"

"You didn't do anything. I breathed too deep." He easily

read the disbelief in her eyes. "Seriously. That's why they gave me that thing." He scowled at the hateful plastic contraption on the coffee table. It was a sort of tube with a ball inside, markings on the outside, and a spout he was supposed to blow into every hour and get the ball to hit the higher marks. He did it once after he got home and ended up having a coughing fit that filled his chest with excruciating pain.

"Do you need some ibuprofen?"

"I could probably use some." He knew she wanted to do something tangible to feel helpful, so he'd do what she wanted, even though they were useless. He normally didn't care for taking medication, but he sure wished they had given him something a little stronger than over the counter pills that did nothing to get through these first couple of days.

He dutifully swallowed two tablets and washed them down with most of the glass of water so he could legitimately prove he was staying hydrated.

Summer curled up beside him, but wouldn't lean against him again. He reached over and held her hand.

"You got an official splint. Nice."

"Yeah." He held up his left hand to inspect the metal splint with blue foam padding taped to his ring finger. "It's bulky, but it's easier to deal with than having two fingers out of commission." He nudged her with his elbow and teased, "At least I haven't convinced you to marry me yet. They would have had to cut my ring off."

She gasped, then laughed, which was exactly the response he was hoping for. "I can't believe you said that."

"Come here." He tugged on her arm.

She hesitated. "I don't want to hurt you."

"Ah. So you *will* marry me." He pulled her close.

"Not with a lame proposal like that."

"All I have to do is propose better? I can do that."

"No way. You're hideous."

"Yeah, well, Beast got Belle."

Summer rolled her eyes and snorted. "Yeah, because he had that huge library and talking candlesticks."

"Is that what it takes? Because I'll go build library shelves right now." He leaned forward like he was getting up.

"You'll do no such thing."

"Can I see your phone?"

"Sure." She handed it over.

Ben typed in a search.

"What are you doing?"

He showed her the screen. "I'm coming up empty finding you a talking candlestick. Is a singing teapot from eBay close enough?"

"Ben." She took her phone back and set it on the far arm of the couch.

"Hey, whatever it takes. Maybe I'll trick your dad into snatching one of my roses."

"You don't have any roses."

"I'll improvise. He can snatch one of my ferns."

"Those are your mother's ferns, and she would hunt him down. As much as she likes me, she'd never accept me as a fair trade."

"That's probably true." He pointed the remote at the television and clicked until he found what he was looking for.

"What are you doing?"

"Getting ideas."

Beauty and the Beast started playing.

He said, "Do you think I could get the townsfolk to join me in a song and dance number?"

"Not until you're healed, at least."

Ben hugged her against his side. "I'm glad you're here."

"Me, too."

"If I didn't have a fat lip, I'd kiss you."

She snickered. "If you didn't have a fat lip, I'd let you."

"Oh, I know you would."

"Seriously? You're awfully confident for being damaged goods."

He laughed at that, and pressed a hand to his chest to ease the burst of ache. "Are you trying to kill me?"

"Not until I'm the beneficiary on your life insurance."

"Cold and calculating. I like it. And I like you."

She blushed a little. "I tolerate you."

He chuckled.

"I guess I like you a little bit." She held her index finger and thumb about an inch apart.

A few minutes later, she heaved a deep sigh.

"What's up?" he asked.

She waved a hand, encompassing him from top to bottom. "This. It's a heck of a way to get out of making me your super-secret special meatballs."

"I already bought everything to make them. If you sign a non-disclosure, I'll show you how to make them."

"Did you get rolls so we can make meatball subs?"

"Pssht, of course."

"And provolone cheese?"

"Have you no faith in me, woman?"

"Just making sure."

He smirked. "A-ha!"

"What?"

"I just cracked the code."

"Oh, really?"

"Yeah. Beast had a library and talking decorations to make Belle fall in love with him. I've got lobster mac and cheese and meatballs to win you over."

Summer rolled her eyes. "Don't count your meatballs before they hatch, mister."

"I'm not. I think the lobster mac and cheese did it. The meatballs will just seal the deal."

She laughed. "I just might kiss you anyway."

His heart did a little flip flop when she did.

Chapter Thirty-Eight

No surprise, the meatballs were delicious. In fact, Summer had the last bowl of them warmed up for lunch on Wednesday. They were that amazing kind of food that was easy to make a massive batch of, and so delicious they were great for lunches for several days.

She speared the last bite and savored it as she updated the profit and loss statement with some new receipts.

The week had been blessedly quiet. Isaac's team was having the fake reviews removed, and no new ones had shown up. It felt like it was taking forever, but their rating was back up to two stars and climbing steadily as the fake reviews were taken down. Not that two stars were great, but she could breathe easier than when it sat at one star.

Ben was healing quite nicely. The bruises on his face were already fading around the edges, to that awful yellow-green, but it was progress. He was getting bored, as evidenced by his constant random text messages.

Diane had banished him from his office for two weeks. Summer knew he'd only make it one, and then even Diane wouldn't be able to keep him from going in and at least puttering around his office.

Her phone vibrated with an incoming call. She wiped her mouth and tossed the napkin in the trash. Her hand froze midway to picking up the phone.

The screen showed the name with three devil emojis.

Nina.

"What do you want?" Summer snapped into the phone.

"Call off your dogs!"

Summer had no idea what she was talking about, but she wasn't about to tell Nina that.

"Please. Summer, I'm begging you. What do I need to do?"

"I think you've done plenty already," Summer answered.

"Look, I may have gone a little too far, but you've ruined my *life*."

"I haven't done anything to you."

"All you had to do was stay with Michael Mastriano and everything would have been great for all of us! He's got more money than Bill Gates and he's smoking hot. Why, Summer? Why couldn't you just stick to the plan?"

Summer bit her tongue.

"Fine, okay, I'm sorry. I shouldn't have posted on your stupid little business page."

She remained silent. If she had any idea how to record the call, she would, but she didn't.

"What can I do?" Nina sounded desperate. "I can't afford these lawsuits!"

Lawsuits? What? Wait, plural? As in more than one lawsuit? Summer coldly said, "I fail to see how this is my problem."

Nina started to cry. Really, authentically cry. "Summer, please. What can I do to get you to cancel these lawsuits?"

Maybe Reesa had gotten a lawyer involved? In any event, Summer went along with it. "I'll need to think about it. A good start would be taking down all the fake reviews."

"Fine. Consider it done."

"I won't consider it done until I see that it's done."

"Okay, but this is going to take me forever," Nina whined.

"You got them all posted in a day, you can take them all down in a day." Summer didn't know exactly how long it took, but she didn't really care. "*All* of them, Nina. Every review on every site. Start by deleting the ones on my brother's business and my sister's business and then do mine... all of them. Every. Last. One. And don't be stupid, Nina. I have screenshots and I know how to count. And so do my lawyers," she added for good measure.

"Even the ones about Reesa? You should be happy about those after what she did to you."

Summer couldn't care less about Reesa. But Kayla still worked there, and it would make her life a little easier. "Even the ones about Reesa."

"Okay, okay. Then you'll call them off?"

"Then I'll *consider* it." She hung up.

Now she just had to find out what the heck Nina was talking about.

Her phone dinged with a text message.

Ben sent her a picture of an empty plate.

> There went the last of my meatballs. You did a great job.

She texted him back a picture of her empty bowl.

> Mine are gone, too. Use some of your vacation to plan another menu.

VACATION????

He sent a string of shocked-face emojis.

> Glad you're feeling better.

I'm climbing the walls.

> Sorry about your luck, spider monkey, but some of us are trying to work.

Are you coming over tonight?

> Of course. I have news.

News?

This was too much for a text message. She picked up the phone and called him to fill him in and he told her about George's Chicago lawyer friend.

"I'll call George and see what went down." He sounded excited. Probably because it gave him something to do.

"Yes, please. I'm dying to know. Whatever it was, it really got her attention." Once they got off the phone, she called her parents over to The Shoppes. She met them in the lobby and updated them along with Gavin and Jillian.

Jillian's brows pinched inward. "Are you sure it was from George's friend? Didn't Isaac mention he might be getting his legal team involved as well?"

"Oh. Now that you say that, I think he did. I'll call him and let you all know what he says. Either way, hopefully this means she takes them all down. I told her to start with yours." She motioned to Gavin and Jillian.

Jillian looked surprised, which just irritated her.

She bit her tongue instead of reminding her sister that she

wasn't the villain of her story and never had been. Instead of engaging at all, she went back upstairs to the office to call Isaac.

Chapter Thirty-Nine

Ben had overdone it. He was bored out of his mind. He'd cleaned the kitchen and bathroom and ran the vacuum in the bedroom, which was probably the last straw for his aching chest. He popped a couple of ibuprofen and downed a glass of water, then sat on the recliner to watch some *Judge Judy* reruns.

He'd called Diane to ask if there was anything going on he needed to know about and she hung up on him. He took it as a good sign everything was running as it should be.

Judge Judy had just rolled her eyes and told a litigant he was peeing on her leg when the door opened and Summer came in, all smiles.

He paused the show. "You look happy."

"I feel like a thousand pound elephant has been lifted off my shoulders."

"That's great." He moved over to the couch so they could sit close together. "Fill me in."

"Apparently George's friend wasn't the only lawyer who got involved."

"Huh?" How was that possible?

"Isaac. He sicced the Frazier Industries attorneys on her. He emailed me a copy of the packet they sent her."

Ben let out a low whistle. "A whole packet?"

"Oh, yeah. They cited chapter and verse all the laws she'd violated with libel and defamation and fraud. It even talks about suing her civilly as well as involving law enforcement and having her charged criminally. It would have scared me, too. Isaac had them call George's friend and apparently he'd sent a similar letter, but no packet."

"Slacker."

Summer giggled. "Right? So she was getting it from two big law firms and it got her attention."

"Good."

She held up her wrist and tapped her watch. "As of four o'clock, all the fake reviews are gone from all the sites for Gavin and Jillian, and a lot of them are down on ours."

"That's great."

"I feel like I can breathe a little bit."

"I can tell. Your eyes are brighter." He brushed a stray lock of hair behind her ear.

"How are you feeling? You're making a face. Is your rib hurting?"

"Yeah, I overdid it."

"Benjamin Matthew."

"Wow, did you learn that from my mom?"

She crossed her arms. "I know you're desperate to do something, but you're going to end up laying yourself up even longer if you don't rest and heal."

"You really did get that from Mom, didn't you?" He'd heard the exact same speech not even two hours earlier.

"Don't deflect."

He leaned back against the cushion and conceded. "You're right. I learned my lesson."

"I just want you to get better."

"I am getting better." He held up a hand. "Okay, okay. I know. I'll be a good boy and stop pushing it."

"Please do." She snuggled against his side and rested her arm across his stomach, careful to avoid bumping his rib.

He breathed in the scent of her shampoo. "You'll sleep good tonight."

"I hope so. I'm exhausted."

Those were the last words she said before nodding off. He turned the volume down and watched a few more episodes of *Judge Judy*.

Summer stirred against him and woke just as Judy chastised a litigant for withholding payment from her wedding planner after the planner had done all the work.

"One of my brides made noises about her dad not paying us if we didn't cow to her bridezilla demands. Reesa put a stop to that pretty quick by calling the dad. After that, she was much more reasonable."

"What kind of wedding do you want?"

"Small. Family and actual friends."

"Do you want to get married at the farm?"

She leaned back and grinned up at him. "Are you kidding? Have you seen the reviews that place has?"

He laughed along with her, and a weight was lifted off his shoulders as well. He'd been more worried about her than he had been about himself. She was absolutely feeling better if she could joke about the situation, and that made him feel better.

He said, "We'll have to get married in the next fifty-three weeks."

"What? Why?"

It wasn't lost on him that she hadn't said no. "Do you remember that summer when you were fifteen? And we said that if we weren't married by the time we were forty, we'd marry each other?"

"You missed that boat. I'm already forty-one."

He raised an eyebrow. "Yeah, but I'm only thirty-nine. I turn forty next week."

"You better get busy building that library, then. See if you can entice me to live in your castle forever."

"I love you, Summer." There. He'd said it out loud, putting his heart in her hands.

She stared up at him for a long time, her blue eyes wide and locked on his. She whispered, "I love you, too."

He put a finger under her chin and lifted her face up so he could kiss her. He'd build the library – heck, he'd build the whole castle – with his bare hands if that's what she wanted.

Chapter Forty

The following Saturday was the perfect specimen of fall days. Summer breathed in the crisp autumn-smelling air. The noon sky was brilliant blue, the perfect backdrop for the remaining orange and yellow leaves that were at the end of their peak. She pushed the button to roll two of the doors up in Creekside Hall.

The slight breeze rustled the tablecloths.

"Is everything ready?" Gavin asked.

"Yup, we just need the cake."

"It's right there." He pointed to the table, where a large white box sat.

Calvin Cooper set up the lunch buffet and Jillian finished arranging the balloons and flowers. A large "HAPPY BIRTH-DAY" banner hung on the wall behind the cake table.

Friends and family streamed into the space, laughing and hugging and setting gifts and envelopes on the table beside the cake.

Gavin looked at his phone. "They're pulling in now. Everybody get ready."

Everyone faced the door expectantly.

Susie and Charlie came in first.

As soon as Ben came in, everyone yelled, "SURPRISE!"

He laughed and blushed a little. "You guys."

"Welcome to forty, old man," Jenna teased.

"Jenna!" Ben ran over and picked his sister up in a massive bear hug, then set her down and pressed a hand to his chest. "Still sore."

He hugged Taylor and Kyler with a bit less force, then hugged George.

"I can't believe you guys are here."

Summer stood off to the side until he held his hand out for her. "Are you responsible for this?"

"Me?" she said with wide-eyed innocence and held her thumb and forefinger an inch apart. "Just a little bit. It was mostly your mom. Are you surprised?"

"I mean, the full parking lot kind of gave it away, but yes, until we pulled in I thought it was just a little family thing." He kissed the top of her head. "Thank you. I love you."

Summer beamed. He said that a lot and she'd never get tired of it. "Love you, too."

Andi went in the side room and turned on some background music.

Mack and Charlie stood off to the side chatting.

People started looking a little restless, so Summer took her cue. She winked at Ben, then left him to go to the center of the room. "Okay, everyone, you can grab some food and find a seat. Let's eat!"

The meal was full of laughter and stories about Ben's antics growing up. Most of the stories involved Gavin.

Summer sat beside him, just watching and wondering why it had taken her so long to realize how perfect he was for her. It must have been one of those "absence makes the heart grow fonder" things, because after the distance of miles and years, she never wanted to be away from him again.

When the meal was over, Gavin proudly unveiled the cake, a three-tier brown ombre masterpiece. The top layer had a dark brown icing with chocolate drip at the edge. It was topped with chopped peanut butter cups.

"Okay, folks, we have options. The top layer is peanut butter cake with peanut butter frosting. Ben's favorite."

"Yum!" Ben yelled.

The second layer was a chocolate cake with peanut butter frosting, and the bottom layer was a yellow cake lightly marbled with chocolate, iced with vanilla frosting.

"Mmm, something for everyone," Summer said.

Gavin called Ben over to join him.

Ben grabbed him in a side-hug. "Thank you. This is amazing. I almost hate to cut it." He looked up to the group. "*Almost.*"

Everyone laughed.

Gavin snickered as he said, "Sorry, buddy, I was afraid of putting that many candles on it. So here." He pulled out a cupcake with 4 and 0 numbered candles on it. He lit them.

Susie started singing and everyone joined in.

"Make a wish," Andi called.

Ben met Summer's eyes and blew the candles out.

Hours later, the crowd had gone. Mack and Andi were putting tables away while Jillian and Gavin boxed up the few remaining pieces of cake. Summer tied the trash bag shut and set it near the door to take to the dumpster.

Ben picked an unopened gift off the table and pulled Summer out the door onto the patio. The air had a slight chill.

"Thank you for today."

"You're welcome. Happy birthday."

"I have a present for you."

"Do you not understand how birthdays work?" she teased.

"I bought this the day after our *Pirates* date." He handed her the box wrapped in silver paper.

"Ben," she breathed. "What did you do?"

"Open it."

Her heart pounded. She knew what it was but didn't want to assume she knew what it was in case it wasn't what she hoped it was.

She balled up the wrapping and shoved it in the pocket of her jeans. The lid slipped off easily, revealing a black velvet box. Her hand trembled as she pulled it out.

Ben took the thin white box from her and tossed it on the floor just inside the door. "I'll pick it up."

She laughed nervously.

Ben gently took the box and got down on one knee. He popped the lid open, but her eyes were on his. "Summer Marie Sullivan. I love you and I want to spend the rest of my life with you. Will you marry me?"

Tears blurred her vision. "Yes! Of course I will!" She bent to kiss him as their families cheered and clapped.

"Are you going to look at it?"

She gasped. The pink diamond solitaire set in a silver band took her breath away. It was the most perfect ring she'd ever seen. If she had been able to pick from every ring in the whole world, this is the one she would have chosen.

Just like this man.

She never wanted to relive the events of the past few months, but finding her way to Ben made it worth all the pain.

Ben stood and pulled her close. "I'd pick you up and spin you around, but…" He gestured to his rib.

"But you're a feeble old man," she said, laughing.

"A feeble old man who got his birthday wish. I'll take it."

They both laughed as they kissed to seal the deal.

Epilogue

In the weeks after the mess with Nina was cleaned up, bookings started flowing in. Isaac's suggestions for where to focus advertising were paying off in spades. They were only a week away from their first vendor event, and everything was coming together nicely.

Summer had wisely followed Isaac's advice and sat with her mom to map out the upcoming year. They decided to schedule two vendor events that would hopefully become annual occurrences. One in the spring and one at the very beginning of December. From there, they looked at holidays and local events and chose two primary weekends a month for weddings, with a selection of back up dates and dates for small events.

In April, they only made room for one wedding.

Hers and Ben's.

She decided to continue living at her parents' instead of spending the money on rent for a handful of months. It would have been a waste anyway, since she spent most of her free time at Ben's.

They put a second desk in the office. Her mom sat at it the

Tuesday before Thanksgiving, checking receipts against the profit and loss statement so they'd be ahead of the game by the end of the year and could just hand everything over to the accountant in early January.

"Are you and Ben going to be here Thursday?"

"Yes. He said his parents always have Thanksgiving dinner at suppertime, so we'll get to have double the food coma."

Andi chuckled. "You're in a food coma half the time anyway. I had no idea Ben was such a good cook. Those meatballs he makes! No wonder you ask for them all the time. What does he do to make them so good?"

"I've been sworn to secrecy."

"Well, I think I'm about done for the day because I'll be cooking all day tomorrow. How about you?"

"Yup. Ben and I'll be making pies all day." She was glad they'd agreed to take a mini-vacation from work. The farm would be closed from Wednesday through Sunday so they could have Thanksgiving and some much needed time off to rest and recharge. "We're getting all the groceries tonight. Wish me luck, because I'm sure the store will be bananas."

She drove to Ben's house and went inside. "Honey, I'm home," she called.

He came out of the hallway with a confused look on his face. "There's something weird in the bathroom."

"What is it?"

"I think you should see for yourself."

She dropped her jacket and purse on the chair and went back the hall. The bathroom door was shut, but there was a strange scratching noise. She slowly turned the knob and pushed the door open a few inches. Four curious eyes popped into the space.

It took her a second to understand what she was seeing.

The orange kitten stepped on his sister's white head and

strolled out of the bathroom. He rubbed against her leg and headed toward the living room like he owned the place. The white kitten with one black ear followed her brother, meowing loudly at his audacity.

She walked behind them, laughing with pure joy as they inspected everything.

"Since you named him Storm, I thought it was fitting to call her Rain."

"I love that." She jerked her gaze up to his. "Wait. How'd you know I named him?"

"You let it slip one time. Maybe twice."

"Oh."

Storm suddenly popped to his tippy toes with his back arched and poofed up his tail. He bounced sideways at his sister, then sprinted away into the kitchen. His little feet scrabbled on the tile as he rounded the island.

Rain sat down and primly licked her paw like she was too dignified to put on such a display.

"This is going to be so much fun."

Ben agreed. "By the way, I went to the grocery store this afternoon and I think I got all the stuff for your pies. You should probably double check in case I missed anything and we have to run back."

She wrapped her arms around his middle. "Thank you." She rested her head against his chest and listened to his heartbeat, strong and steady like always.

"You good?"

"I'm great. Just listening to your heart and thinking about how you're so calm. My safe harbor in the storms of chaos. You always help me get everything back under control."

Storm zipped past and leaped up to scale the curtain.

He chuckled softly. "Control is an illusion."

"Don't I know it."

Up next: Book Two of the Willow Creek trilogy

When a blast from the past turns baker Gavin Sullivan's life upside down, will he repeat his same mistakes, or will he ultimately get to have his cake and eat it, too?

Order Recipe for Disaster today!

Also by Carrie Jacobs

HICKORY HOLLOW (Can be read in any order):

Drunk on a Plane

Caller Number Nine

The Boy Next Door

Luck of the Draw

Cat Burglar

Mending Fences

Two Tickets to Paradise

Bad Advice

Where There's a Will (novella)

STAND ALONE:

The Bucket List

WILLOW CREEK:

#1 Everything's Under Control

#2 Recipe for Disaster

#3 Forget Me Not

For details about all of my books, visit my website. For exclusive sneak peeks, behind-the-scenes information, and much more, sign up for my newsletter at carriejacobs.com.

Author's Note

Dear Reader,

I can hardly believe this is my TENTH published novel! I hope you enjoyed Summer and Ben's story as much as I enjoyed writing it. I can't wait to spend more time (two more books!) in Willow Creek with the Sullivans.

I can identify with Summer on a lot of levels. I'm a little bit of a control freak with some major anal retentive tendencies (if you know me, quit laughing). I've never set a laptop on fire, but I won't say it'll never happen.

Next up is Gavin's story, Recipe for Disaster, and then we'll wrap up the trilogy with Jillian's story in Forget Me Not.

In this book, I mentioned Mr. Sticky's. Y'all, this place is REAL and it is PHENOMENAL. If you like sticky buns and you're anywhere near Mechanicsburg, PA, you need to give them a try. mrstickysofcentralpa.com

To keep up with all the latest updates and news, be sure to sign up for my newsletter at carriejacobs.com! You'll get exclusive sneak peeks, behind-the-scenes info, notice of upcoming releases, and all that jazz. You can also follow me on Facebook facebook.com/writercarriejacobs for updates, notice of my upcoming events and more importantly, pictures of my furry editorial assistants.

If you enjoyed Everything's Under Control and have a moment to spare, leaving a review online would be very helpful to me. (Even if you didn't buy it online, you can still leave a review.)

Until next time ~ control is an illusion! 😉

Best,

Carrie

About the Author

Carrie's love of storytelling began in early childhood and never wavered as time marched onward. She reads in pretty much every genre imaginable, but found her writing happy place in small town contemporary romance and romantic comedy.

From that love came Hickory Hollow, a mashup of her hometown and places she's either visited or would like to. Her favorite part of Hickory Hollow? The residents don't have to drive an hour to get to Target, like she does in real life.

Carrie lives in beautiful central Pennsylvania with her very own romcom hero and thoroughly spoiled furry editorial assistants.

Connect with Carrie through her newsletter or social media!

Website: carriejacobs.com